Season's Grievings

Season's Grievings

Tales of Travel Horror

Edited by

Emily J. Weisenberger

ROF Publishing House name and logo are trademarks of
AAF Creative Studio

First Printing: 2025
ISBN: 978-1-7336896-2-5 (Print)
ISBN: 978-1-7336896-3-2 (eBook)

10 9 8 7 6 5 4 3 2 1

TO VICTOR, WHO LISTENS

Acknowledgements

There is nothing like a short story anthology to remind you to be grateful for community. For community that is built between the authors and editors and artists, of course, and the ripples of it out further to the readers, and even further to the readers, friends, or bed partners who are kept up late at night hearing about a story they never read (never even wanted to read but now know the whole plot). Thanks to all those involved in putting this anthology together and all the way to those who will have to hear about it when they're trying to fall asleep. A big thanks to Ah Xul, Anastasia, Lauren, and Lyl and especially to Nico, my friend and mentor.

I am a late convert to the horror genre. As a kid and into adulthood, reading dark stories led to dark, festering fears about unknowable dangers. But to conquer a thing, you have to face it. Reading and writing dark stories is how you can turn unknowable dangers into things known and dealt with. At the end of a dark story, the character—and you—has changed, but they've also gone on or at least gone out fighting. There is power in those endings. I credit this change in my thinking—empowerment through horror—to Rob Costello and Anna-Marie McLemore's class on writing queer, young adult horror, which they taught through the Highlights Foundation in 2024.

I hope that you, reader, find something in this anthology to shock or scare or challenge you, and when you turn to the final page, you feel the better for having read it.

— Emily J. Weisenberger, August 2025 —

TO OSCAR, XAVIER AND SOLEI

Acknowledgements

My father was many things in his life, but what defined him most was his love of writing, especially his poetry. He loved to read everything he could get his hands on: newspapers, history, political musings, thrillers, sci-fi, and stories of both triumph and failure. He admired writers who could spin stories the way a spider spins a web.

He wrote poetry his entire life, though he only began keeping it in his twenties. Reading his early work now, I catch glimpses of the young man who would one day become my father. Over the years, in countless conversations, he expressed a quiet longing to see his poetry published. Like many writers, he doubted himself. He believed his work might not measure up to the authors he so deeply admired.

After his passing, I decided to give him the one thing he had always wanted. I created ROF Publishing House, named in his honor, to share his work with the world. In 2019, *A Poetic Journey Through Time* was published, and it remains available on Amazon and Apple Books.

Every time I see his book or speak with someone who has read it, I feel his presence. I sense his pride. If he were alive today, I know he would pull his book from the shelf with a smile and say,

"Look at this book. That's my work."

For a time, I wasn't sure what more to do with this publishing company. Then the amazing Nico Bell asked me a simple question: "Hey, do you wanna do a book?" That one question not only opened the door to independent publishing for me but gave me the permission to walk through it. Now, as I think about the future of this company, what I want it to be and how I want it to grow, I think of my dad. I want ROF Publishing House to be a home for incredibly talented authors, a place where they can spin stories and create outstanding books. I want readers to feel the excitement of discovering them.

Most of all, I want the authors I work with to be able to go to their own shelves, pull out their book with pride, and say:

"Look at this book. That's my work."

— Ah Xul Fuentes, August 2025 —

Trigger Warning

This anthology contains horror stories with dark elements, and intense, sometimes unsettling subject matter. While each story is fictional, the emotions they evoke may be very real.

Please read with care and prioritize your well-being.

To review the list of stories and their trigger warning, turn to the last page.

TABLE OF CONTENTS

KAY HANIFEN

Kay Hanifen was born on a Friday the 13th and once lived for three months in a haunted castle. So, obviously, she had to become a horror writer.

Her work has appeared in over one hundred anthologies and magazines. Her first anthology as an editor, Till the Yule Log Burns Out, was published in 2024. Her first novel, The Last Ballard, debuted in 2025. When she's not consuming pop culture with the voraciousness of a vampire at a 24-hour blood bank, you can usually find her with her black cats or at kayhanifenauthor.wordpress.com.

Instagram: @katharinehanifen
The Last Ballard: https://www.miravallebooks.com/books/thelastballard

THE CHRISTMAS SCARECROW
BY KAY HANIFEN

"Uncle—Aunt Stella, do you want to build a snowman?" Maria asked, sing-songing to the tune of that Disney song. My niece was ten and we'd always gotten along. She was sweet, still getting used to my new name and pronouns but trying … which was more than I could say for most of the family. She gazed at me expectantly, already dressed in her snowsuit. Lizzie, her little sister, stood beside her, struggling to put on her gloves. The rest of the cousins and siblings were scattered to the winds—some already outside while others watched TV, played video games, or sat glued to their phones. Not that I was judging the latter. My phone was my number one escape for the awkwardness all around me. It's fun being the only trans person in a huge, Catholic family. Each year, we gathered in the ancestral family farmhouse, the only place large enough for all of us, and tried our best not to kill one another for two weeks.

I set my phone down. "Sure, let me just get dressed."

Her dad, Harry, cleared his throat. "I don't think that's a good idea. I'd rather you weren't alone with my daughters."

Oh here we go. I got to my feet, stretching lazily, like a cat. Harry had never liked me, not before my transition and certainly not after. He hated it when I acted unbothered, so I did just that. "You're welcome to join us. Better than sitting on your butt drinking beer while Janet's slaving away in the kitchen."

Maria's eyes widened as her mouth dropped open. "Ooooh," she mocked. Did I mention how much I loved this kid?

A vein bulged in his temple. Honestly, what did Janet see in him? Of my many siblings, I was closest with her, but sometimes, I wondered what her taste in men said about her.

3

"Fine. I'll suit up too," he grumbled, as though it physically pained him to spend time with his children.

I honestly don't know what he expected me to do to them out in the front yard. Probably infect them with the woke mind virus or something. I threw my snowsuit on and met the girls at the door. Maria was frowning while Lizzie sang a loop of the Disney song. It was off-key and had a little lisp from her missing front teeth, so, you know, it was adorable.

"What's with the sour face?" I asked, ruffling Maria's hair. "Because remember that you'd better watch out, and you'd better not pout."

"Mémère told me a story," she said. Oh boy, this was an infamous one. My grandmother—her great-grandmother—was from Alsace, France, and she loved to scare her grandchildren with stories of a monster at Christmastime: Hans Trapp, the evil scarecrow. Legend has it that he was a knight who made a deal with the devil and got turned into an immortal scarecrow for his crimes against the monks in the area. Now, he wanders the earth, capturing naughty children, and shoving them into sacks as punishment. It was a mix between Krampus and a real-life historical figure who was excommunicated for being a massive asshole.

"Hans Trapp?" I guessed.

Her eyes widened. "You know him?"

I laughed. "Not personally, of course. Mémère scared the naughty out of me with him when I was your age. You have nothing to worry about, though. You're a good kid."

Maria's frown returned as she pointed out the window. "Then why is that in the fields?"

Squinting, I followed her finger to the shape of a scarecrow in the snowy distance. "They must have forgotten to take it down during the harvest."

She shook her head. "It was farther away yesterday and even farther the day before. It keeps moving closer."

Before I could formulate a response, Harry appeared. "Alright. You wanted to build a snowman?" He glanced snidely at me. "Assuming that he doesn't decide to become a snow-woman instead."

I rolled my eyes at the jab. I swear, these people only ever have one joke. "We should get started so we'll be done by dinner."

"Sure, whatever," he grunted before sitting on the porch with his spiked eggnog. Would it kill him to show some interest in his daughters?

"So, should we start from the top down or the bottom up?" I asked.

Both girls giggled. "That's silly, Uncle Stella," Lizzie said. It wasn't totally right, but she was getting there. She was also six, so if she could get my name right, then Harry and Janet certainly could. "If you start with the top, it'll drop."

I smacked my forehead. "Right, duh. Silly me. I'll get the bottom. Maria, you do the middle, and Lizzie, you make the head. Got it?"

Maria saluted. "Yes ma'am." The use of *ma'am* earned a scoff from Harry, which we both dutifully ignored.

Grabbing a handful of snow, I began to pack it into a ball. It was the perfect snowman snow. Rather than powder, it was wet and heavy, making it easy to mold. I could practically roll it like carpet.

After a few minutes, Harry seemed to grow bored, so he went inside, but made a point of watching from the window. I, in turn, made a point of always being in view. He could say nothing against me.

"Why doesn't Daddy like you?" Lizzie asked as she rolled her head. It was nearly the size of an infant, and she was struggling to lift it. We would have to assemble the snowman soon.

Before I could answer, Maria answered for me. "It's because she's transgender, and Daddy doesn't like that. He thinks it's wrong and bad."

Lizzie furrowed her brows thoughtfully. "Is it?"

We both gazed at Maria expectantly. An anxious feeling curdled my stomach. Kids parrot their parents' views at this age so whatever came next shouldn't be taken too personally. She just shrugged. "One of my classmates was named Sarah at the beginning of the year and is now named Steven. He's happier as Steven." She picked up the head, her gaze meeting mine. "And I think you're a lot happier as my aunt than my uncle. I loved you as my uncle, so I think I'll love you as my aunt too."

Tears blurred my vision as I pulled my niece into a hug. She stiffened in surprise for a moment before relaxing and hugging me back. Never one to be left out, Lizzie joined in for a group hug.

"Hey," Harry barked, slamming the door open. "Don't you fucking touch my daughters." The girls let go as though they just realized they had been touching a burning stove.

7

"It was a hug," I said. "You never objected to me hugging your daughters before."

"Well, that was before …" He gestured to me with my long hair, ugly Christmas sweater, and plaid skirt. "You became this."

"Harry, what's going on?" Janet demanded. From over his shoulder, I could see a small crowd of cousins, siblings, aunts, and uncles forming to gaze at the spectacle.

"Your *brother* was touching our girls," he growled. There were gasps and murmurs through the crowd. This was a mistake. Most of the family had been politely passive-aggressive, so I thought I could take it, but with the way they were all turning against me, I was better off staying home.

"I just said I loved her, and she hugged me," Maria said. "That's all. Nothing bad."

He scoffed. "You wouldn't understand, Maria. You don't know what he could do to you if he wanted."

She straightened, her chin jutting out defiantly. "I understand enough to know that you're being a bully, Dad." There were some gasps from the younger kids. Maria wasn't one who normally defied her parents.

8

"Another word out of you, and Santa won't be coming to our house tonight. He hates naughty children who talk back to their parents."

Maria gasped as though she'd been punched. That was a low blow, even for him. Tears filled her and Lizzie's eyes.

"Harry," Janet said, "you're making a scene."

He turned to address the crowd growing behind him. "Is no one else concerned about your brother and his … his *perversions* around our children?" Most of the family averted their eyes, but there were a few murmurs of agreement.

"What on earth is going on here?" Mémère exclaimed, emerging from the kitchen like a flour-covered goddess. She spoke with an interesting mixture of a French and German accent particular to Alsace, which bordered the two nations. My grandmother was nearly a hundred and bent like a question mark, but she commanded the crowd like a general. The family was immediately cowed. All but Harry, of course.

"I'm just protecting my daughters," he said, glaring at me.

"From who?" She swept her hand in an arc. "I don't see any dangers here. Only family. Now, who will help me in the kitchen? You can't leave an old woman to put a meal on the table all by herself."

This was the crowd's signal to disperse, leaving only me, Harry, Mémère, Janet, and the girls. Lizzie burst into tears and ran into her mom's arms. "I don't want to be on the naughty list," she wept.

Mémère patted the top of her head. "Don't worry, *ma belle*. You and your sister are very good little girls. Now, it looks as though you were working on a snowman?"

"I'll let you guys finish up," I said, edging towards the door.

Maria grabbed my hand. "I want you to finish it with me."

Ignoring Harry's stormy expression, I looked to Janet, who nodded her assent, but she looked reluctant. "I'll help," my sister said. "If that's okay with you." I couldn't tell if she was asking Harry or our grandmother.

Mémère smiled, revealing her gold teeth. "I have enough hands in the kitchen. Just be washed up by dinner." With that, she disappeared inside. Harry gave us one last disapproving look before following her.

The moment the door shut, Janet seemed to relax, her shoulders no longer up by her ears. "I'm sorry about Harry, Jo—Stella."

I didn't look at her, instead helping Maria stack the middle of the snowman on the bottom and fill in the cracks for stability. "It's about what I expected from him."

"It's still bullying," Maria muttered.

I flashed her a smile. "I've faced scarier bullies than your dad," I replied just loudly enough for her to hear. She grinned back at me.

Janet squeezed her arms to her chest as though trying to create the facsimile of a hug. "It's no excuse, though. He's … he's changed. When he lost his job, he'd spent a lot of time online and started spouting bizarre theories. I thought it would get better once he got back to work, but he's … I don't know …"

"Meaner," Maria supplied for her. "He used to let us paint his nails and play princesses. Now, he just screams at the TV or the computer."

"Sometimes, he scares me." Lizzie's soft voice shattered my heart.

Horror at their words sank in, followed by rage. Harry could bully me all he wanted, but if he was hurting my sister or his children, then I was going to kill him and make sure they never found the body. Taking a slow, calming breath, I got to my feet and approached Janet like she was a wounded animal. "Are you and the girls safe?"

Her eyes widened. "What? God, it's nothing as bad as that. He's just been a jerk. You don't have to worry about us."

What I wanted to say was, *girl, divorce his unwashed ass.* It was on the tip of my tongue, but we'd barely spoken since I came out, and I didn't want to risk breaking this delicate olive branch. So, instead, I smiled, pulling her into a hug and not caring if Harry came out to object again. "We're family. Worrying about each other is what we do."

"I missed you," she said.

That stung in a way I didn't expect. She didn't react poorly to me coming out, but she didn't react well either, going from texting me almost every day to one-word answers to conversations I initiated. But progress was progress. I stepped back. "I've been here the whole time."

"Um, is it just me or is the scarecrow even closer now?" Maria asked, breaking up this heartwarming sisters moment.

"Honey, that's just your—huh." Janet squinted at the scarecrow. "Weird."

I hated to admit it, but Maria was right. The scarecrow had moved. Before, it was a good distance out, but now, I could make out its white beard against its brown clothes. I glanced over at Janet, who had an equally puzzled expression on her face.

"I guess we should check it out," I said reluctantly, though I couldn't place why.

Maria grabbed my arm before I could go more than a few steps. "Haven't you seen a scary movie? The first person to die is always the one who investigates the weird thing." She had a point, of course. This was Horror 101. If there was any chance of this being a murderous scarecrow, then I should run as far as I could in the other direction.

"It's probably a prank by one of your cousins," Janet said. "They've all heard the story of Hans Trapp, and I can think of a few who would love to mess with us like that."

"But what if it isn't?" Lizzie said. "What if Hans Trapp is here to take us away for being naughty?"

"Then he'll have to go through us," I said, throwing an arm around my sister. "We can fight off an old scarecrow if we have to. In the meantime, we'll finish our snowman. He can stand guard to make sure there aren't any mean scarecrows getting in."

Seemingly satisfied by this suggestion, the girls helped us assemble the last parts of the snowman, adding pinecones for eyes, a carrot for the nose, and a series of buttons for the mouth. We wrapped him in a scarf and added sticks for arms. By the time we were done, the sun had fully gone down, and we headed inside for dinner.

Despite the scene Harry made earlier (or, perhaps, because of it), everyone was a lot more civil to me, many making attempts to get my name and pronouns correct. Never let it be said that dislike of a single asshole relative couldn't bring people together. I may have been the black sheep of the family, but everyone knew that Janet could do better than Harry. Unfortunately, divorce was frowned upon in our Catholic family, so she had been trying to stick it out, mostly for the sake of the girls. That said, from what I could tell, they'd probably be happier without him, and Janet seemed to be coming to that conclusion too. With any luck, she would be single by next Christmas.

Dinner was as wonderful as it was every year. Mémère was an amazing cook, drawing from her region's mixture of French and German cuisine. Even the pickiest eaters found something to like at her table, and the first few minutes were spent in quiet appreciation of the food. Slowly, though, conversation began to pick up as we sated our hunger.

"So, Joey," my Uncle Ron said. "What's with the new look?"

There was a collective intake of breath. Everyone knew about my transition at this point—it was difficult not to—but it was still an elephant in the room, one that people politely decided to sidestep. Not Uncle Ron, though. If I was the elephant in the room, then he was the conversational bull in the China shop.

"It's Stella, now, actually," I replied. "I realized a few things about myself and started making changes to better help me look like the way I feel on the inside."

"So, you think you can just say you're something and expect people to go along with it?" he asked, looking like he thought he'd caught me in an impenetrable logical fallacy.

"I mean, you call yourself a successful businessman and entrepreneur, but every business you start goes under within five years," I retorted mildly, earning another collective gasp. Some giggled and *oooh'ed* while others looked horrified. His face turned a deep purple with anger and embarrassment. My attitude since coming out can best be described as do no harm but take no shit. If someone comes out swinging, then I have no problem hitting back.

"Jo—Stella!" Mom admonished, and I appreciated her correcting herself, even if she was angry at me.

I shrugged. "He came for me first."

"Still, be a bit more respectful of your elders," she said, talking to me like I was five.

"As long as he respects me too." I took a bite of Mémère's roasted duck to punctuate my point.

She sighed, but I caught Janet's gaze and gave her a wink. Pursing her lips to hide her amusement, she rolled her sparkling eyes.

"So, what did you all ask Santa for?" I directed the question to the children at the table, who were rarely addressed while the adults talked.

Cousins, nieces, and nephews chimed in with the latest Barbies, video games, and toys I had never heard of but hoped their parents would give them. The thing is that I like kids. They're funny and creative and always eager to better understand the world around them. I considered becoming an elementary school teacher and even started getting my master's in education, but when I had my gender crisis, a different kind of fear also took root. There were a lot of parents like Harry out there. They probably wouldn't want a transfem teacher. They might accuse me of something horrible just because I happened to use the same bathroom as my female students.

I knew I shouldn't let my fears get in the way of my passion, but I still wound up changing my focus to administration. It was far less visible and meant that I wouldn't be completely throwing away the work I had already completed towards my degree. The choice hurt, but it was ultimately for the best.

All things considered, it was as good a Christmas Eve dinner as I could have hoped. Everyone remained civil, and after Uncle Ron, they made a point of using the correct name and pronouns, even if they slipped up from time to time. If anyone stepped out of line, they risked facing the full force of Mémère's glare. The woman was ancient and tiny but still cowed the most terrifying of men.

I helped her clean up after everyone had moved on to the living room and the children were heading to bed in anticipation of Santa's visit. "Thank you, Mémère, for defending me," I said quietly as I scrubbed the dishes.

She sidled up to me, taking the plate I washed in her gnarled fingers. "My Aunt Greta was a nurse at the *Institut für Sexualwissenschaft*. Do you know what that is?"

"The first place in the West to study trans people and give gender reassignment surgery," I replied softly, reverently.

She nodded, her smile revealing her gold teeth. "She came to live with us for a time after the raids and book burnings. I was a little girl at the time, and I did not understand what was happening, just that she was afraid. France, we thought, would be safer than Berlin. But then … well … we were among the first to fall in the blitzkrieg. She joined the resistance but was captured and executed."

"I'm sorry," I said.

Her gaze turned wistful as her mind journeyed to the past. "I hadn't thought of her in years. But when I was really little, my aunt had been my uncle. My parents might have taught me acceptance, but she taught me true courage."

Tears blurred in my eyes. "I wish I could have met her."

Mémère pulled me into a hug. "I wish it too. But I am glad that she never had to live to see it seem as though it was all happening again."

Stepping backwards, she wiped my tears from my cheeks. "There's my brave girl. Be Aunt Greta to your nieces and nephews. They will need the example of someone like you." Pulling my head down, she pressed a kiss to my forehead. "Go to bed. Sleep, and *Père Noël* will come."

I chuckled weakly. "I think I'm a little old for Santa, Mémère."

"You're never too old. Now, off to bed or Hans Trapp might get you. I'll have one of your useless brothers help me clean up the rest."

Giggling, I obeyed, heading out of the kitchen. I realized my mistake when I saw my brothers, uncles, brothers-in-law, and older male cousins were gathered. There were a couple women in the mix, but most were putting the children to bed. All fell silent when I stepped into the room. Alarm bells rang in my head, the kind honed from years of evading school bullies.

I forced a smile. "Well, I'm off to bed."

"This early?" Uncle Ron asked. "Come on, at least have a glass of eggnog."

"Mémère's orders," I replied with a shrug. It was silly to go to bed this early, but she was a hard woman to disobey.

"No offense, but she's old enough to think you're one of the kids," one of my brothers, Bill, said.

"She's sharper than you, Bill," I retorted. "Now, do you have something to say to me, or can you just let me go to bed?"

"Yeah, actually, I do. I—" Harry began, but then there was a knock at the door. We all fell silent, exchanging glances. The family was all accounted for, and there weren't any neighbors around for miles. So, who was knocking at the door?

Another knock. This time more insistent.

I wasn't sure why I was so anxious as I approached the door, but chills sprinted up and down my spine as I unlocked it. The moment I turned the knob, a force powerful enough to knock me over blew open the door. The air left my lungs as I landed flat on my back.

Standing in the doorway was a very tall, old man, one with a long, white beard and a sack slung over one shoulder. For a moment, I thought, *Santa?* But then I registered the straw sticking out of his burlap clothes.

Hans Trapp. The evil Christmas scarecrow. It shouldn't have been possible, but here he was.

Still on my back, I scooted away in a clumsy crab walk, only caring about getting as far from him as possible.

"What the hell is—" Uncle Ron began, but then the scarecrow held a finger to his dry lips.

"I am here for the wicked children," he said, his voice as dry as the straw filling him. The room fell horribly silent, the cracking of the fire in the hearth the only sound. For all their chest thumping about protecting children from supposed predators like me, they were noticeably silent when faced with an actual child predator.

Lizzie, Maria, and all the other kids were upstairs. No matter what happened, I couldn't let him hurt them. I got to my feet and drew myself to my full height. I'm six feet tall, but he had a good foot on me. "There are no wicked children here, Hans Trapp," I said.

"You know this guy?" Bill practically growled, as though *I* were the danger here.

"Just from the stories Mémère told us. You'd know him too if you paid attention," I replied. "He's like Krampus and punishes naughty children." I met his icy gaze again. "But you won't find any here. All the children are sweet, well-behaved, clean, and respectful."

He tilted his head. "That is not entirely true. You are all children of God, are you not?"

My throat went dry at the implication. "You can take adults too."

He smiled, revealing rotting teeth. "Yes, and I see many wicked children of God are among us here tonight."

A murmur rippled through the crowd of family members. "What are you talking about?" Harry demanded, his voice slightly slurred. "We haven't done anything wrong."

His chuckle was like the susurration of wind through tall wheat. "Come now. Can you truly not see your own cruelty? Have you not noticed the way that your children avoid your very presence, how they always leave for the next room and barely say two words to you? Can't you see the way they choose to be kind in spite of you rather than because of you?" He tilted his head, regarding Harry the way one might regard a fly before swatting it.

Harry balked. "You—you don't know what you're saying."

"I am not the Ghost of Christmas Yet to Come. I bring no dire warnings. I am simply here to punish the wicked."

"Aunt Stella?" Maria said from the top of the stairs. Janet was at the bottom. Both mother and daughter's eyes were wide with terror. "Is—is that Hans Trapp?"

He smiled, tilting his head in amusement. "And is that a disobedient child I see? Your mother was putting you to bed."

Maria went pale and let out a terrified whimper.

"Hey, no, you said you weren't here for any of the children," I objected, mostly to keep his attention on me and away from my niece. I heard the rapid sound of footsteps as she ran to hide. Good.

"I said nothing of the sort. I said that even adults are children of God. I will not object to taking away a naughty child." He paused, tilting his head thoughtfully. "Or someone who stands in my way."

"Like hell you will," Harry exclaimed, tottering to his feet. "I don't know who you think you are, and I don't care. You're leaving now."

"Or what, child?" he growled.

Over Janet's protests, Harry threw a punch, aiming— albeit drunkenly—at Hans Trapp. This, as it turned out, was a fatal mistake. Hans Trapp caught his fist, eyeing it with a distant curiosity. Harry began to cough, weakly at first, but then powerful and wracking sounds as he doubled over, his mouth full of straw. He turned to the family as though to ask for help, but he couldn't get the words out as his skin turned to burlap. He took one step, and then two, and then collapsed into a pile of straw.

For a moment, all were silent. And then Janet screamed, waking all of us from our terrified stupor and spurring us into action. The crowd dispersed, fleeing to all corners of the farmhouse. I spotted Hans Trapp grab Uncle Ron, his flesh morphing into straw and burlap.

Mom grabbed me by the arm as I ran past. Her eyes were wild. "The children."

"Right," I said, and then sprinted up the steps. The doors down the hall were opening, revealing the confused and frightened faces of our youngest family members. Some had tears already streaking down their cheeks. "Lock your bedroom doors and hide," I ordered. "Don't come out unless an adult you know tells you it's safe."

They stood frozen, as though unsure if they should listen to the black sheep of the family. Maria broke the frightened silence. "Come on! We can't let Hans Trapp get us." Then, she took Lizzie by the hand, shut the door, and locked it with a click. Room by room, the rest of the children followed suit. Good. They were safe for now.

Screams still resounded through the downstairs as he took my family. Most of those people were assholes and bigots but not even they deserved a fate like that. I had to do something.

In the *Wizard of Oz*, the scarecrow's weakness was fire. Would that apply to Hans Trapp?

Well, most things die when set on fire, so it was worth a shot for that reason alone. I just had to lure him away from the house and the children. After telling them to lock up, I couldn't let the house catch on fire.

An idea forming in my head. I raced down the stairs, grabbing the bourbon used to spike the eggnog as I slipped into the kitchen. The floor was covered in straw, and I tried not to think about the family members I was stepping on as they crunched underfoot. "Sorry Mémère," I muttered as I fed one of her tea towels into the bottleneck.

"He will not try to take you," she said from the shadows, making me jump. "If you hide like the rest of the children, he will pass over you."

"You scared me," I said, putting a hand to my racing heart.

25

She had this odd, unsettling gleam in her eyes. "Go to bed, Stella. He is not here for you."

"How would you know that?" I asked.

She smiled, but it was far from comforting. "Because I told him to use you as the standard for the rest of the adults' wickedness. If they treated you well, they would be spared. But if they bullied you, they would be punished."

"Did … did you summon him?" I didn't want to believe it, but this was the only thing that made sense with what she was saying.

Her expression became indignant even as tears sparkled in her eyes. "Don't you see that it's happening again? I did it to protect you. To protect all of us."

"You couldn't just cut them off like a normal person? Write them out of your will?" I asked, my heart rabbiting in my chest. All my life, I had thought of Mémère as a sweet and dignified old lady, but she had been through a lot. She had survived Nazi occupation and immigrating to the United States, among everything else that occurred in the last ninety years. Something in her must have snapped when she saw the world once again shifting towards fascism.

"Oh, I did that too. But they needed to be taught a lesson first."

I can't say that I relished the idea of riding in to rescue the people who treated me like shit, but as long as people are alive, they still have time to change. Hurting them will have some short-term satisfaction, but it won't do much good in the long run.

"Sorry Mémère," I said. "I can't let you do this." I paused, thinking. "Maybe if you had directed him towards the ones making history repeat, I wouldn't have objected, but—"

"I understand. You are too good, *ma chérie*."

It was strange to me that she would just let me go like that, but I wasn't going to question it too much. I grabbed a lighter and left.

Hans Trapp had moved into the dining room, smiling as he turned Aunt Candace into a straw effigy. "Hey!" I shouted, careful to keep the Molotov cocktail out of his sight.

He looked up and smiled, revealing his rotting teeth. "Leave me. You are not wicked like the others."

"But I am," Janet said, pushing past me.

"What are you doing?" I hissed.

"You're not exactly subtle with the Molotov," she whispered back before raising her head. "I abandoned my sister and turned my back on my principles at the behest of a man I can barely stand. If that isn't wicked, I don't know what is. So come and get me."

With that, she turned on her heel and ran, sprinting for the front door. Hans Trapp followed close behind.

"Damn it, Janet," I muttered, having to stop to light the cocktail. By the time I stepped out the door, he was already clear of the house, thankfully. But he was also gaining on my sister. "Hey! Scarecrow!" I shouted, raising the burning glass.

He stopped to turn around, and I chucked it. The Molotov hit him straight in the chest, catching him on fire like he was made entirely out of kindling, which, if we're being honest, he probably was.

He screamed, and the same blast of magic that bowled me over when he arrived sent me flying again. It knocked me flat on my back, and then I wasn't aware of anything for a while.

***

"Aunt Stella, Aunt Stella, Santa came!" Lizzie exclaimed, jumping on my bed.

I groaned, cracking an eye open. "What?" Then, the events of the night all came back to me. I shot up in bed. "Lizzie! Are you and Maria okay?"

"They're fine," Janet said from the bedroom door. "Maria's just waiting downstairs for Miss Sleepyhead to wake up so we all can finally open presents."

I got out of bed and followed them down the stairs. "Janet, last night—"

She shrugged. "I know as much as you do. He went up in flames, knocked me backwards, and I woke up in bed with Harry by my side. The girls seemed to think that last night was just a weird nightmare. And Harry … well, you'll see."

The moment we stepped into the living room, I understood. Harry took one look at me, and like Ebenezer Scrooge after being visited by the three spirits, his face spread into a wide, excited smile. "Stella!" Jumping to his feet, he pulled me into a hug, followed by Uncle Ron and anyone else who had purposefully misgendered or deadnamed me over the past few days.

"I'm so sorry for being an ass," Harry said. "You saved us all."

I shot Janet a stunned look, but she just shrugged. As the kids tore into their gifts, I approached Mémère. "What's going on?" I asked.

She smiled, suddenly looking decades younger and absolutely delighted with herself. "I did what I said I would. I taught them a lesson in good behavior by having Hans Trapp show them the error of their ways." Reaching over, she squeezed my shoulder. "They were never going to be his for long, but it was still brave of you and your sister to face him."

Our gazes both slid over to Janet, who was admiring Maria's new bead bracelet kit. When she saw us watching, she smiled.

"To love is a choice, even to love your family," Mémère said. "I know some of us make it a hard decision, but I am grateful that you came. Perhaps this lesson from Hans Trapp will stick."

"I hope so," I replied, smiling at the joy on Lizzie's face as she opened a singing Barbie.

Mémère grinned and gave my shoulder one last pat. "Well, if they keep it up, I might even write them back into the will."

CAT VOLEUR

Cat Voleur is a writer of dark, speculative fiction and co-host of the Nic F'n Woo Cage Cast. Cat is also a recurring guest on Creepy and Geeky. Which can be found on YouTube and Spotify.

When she's not creating or consuming morbid content, you can find her watching horror movies with her army of rescued felines.

<u>Socials</u>
Twitter: @Cat_Voleur
Instagram: catvoleur
Bluesky: catvoleur

DAWN TO BREAK
BY CAT VOLEUR

It was as dark as it could ever be in the North at winter. Each and every speck of light was reflected back toward the sky from the dazzling, unbroken snow that was spread across the field before the two women.

"Will you sit with me?" Millie asked.

"It's almost dawn," June said. "And we're almost there. We should keep going." Something in her was desperate to keep going.

"Please? I know you're tired."

June *was* tired. It had been a long night and an even longer walk. She was afraid if she sat down, her weary bones would not have it in them to stand again. All the same, she could not resist when she saw the gentle look in her lover's eyes. This was the sort of spontaneity she had always wanted in her partner; she could hardly deny it now.

"For just a few minutes," she said as she sat down atop the crest of the hill.

"Perfect," Millie said. She settled into the snow beside June, wrapping an arm around her, holding her close. Even through the thick, bulky layers of her winter attire, Millie felt warm. "I want to watch the sunrise with you."

The scenery was perfect, but the silence wore June down far quicker than the cold winds. Silence carried thoughts, contemplation, and the nagging sense she was supposed to be home already.

"Can we talk?"

"Talk about what?" Millie asked.

"Anything," June said. "Please?"

Millie pulled her even closer so that her head was resting against the big, puffy jacket. June leaned into the pull and repositioned so that her head was entirely in Millie's lap, staring up at her with admiration. She was not prepared for the next question that was posed to her.

"Did you know they used to tell ghost stories at Christmas?"

"Did they?"

"Mhmm. In England, I think. Victorian England, before electricity. When the nights would get really long, right around the winter solstice, there were more dark hours that couldn't be worked through. They needed ways to pass the time. So they told ghost stories."

It was exactly the sort of morbid fact that Millie would know, and June could not help but tease her lightly. "You'd tell ghost stories all the time if you could."

"I can," she teased right back.

"Tell me one now."

"One what?"

"A ghost story."

Millie's gloved hand stroked June's hair. "Are you sure that's how you want to start your Christmas? We're not in Victorian England."

"Let's pretend."

Millie gave her an almost somber smile. "We'll pretend, then."

"Good. Now, go."

She sighed before she spoke again. "Did you know these woods are haunted?"

"How would you know? You've never been out here before."

"You don't know what I've done. I'm a Victorian storyteller."

Millie said it so sincerely, with her Boston accent, that June could not help but laugh. The sound was bells tinkling into the crisp air. She was red faced and breathless by the time Millie stopped her.

"Do you want to hear the story or not?"

June took a few more breaths and steadied herself by looking up into the charcoal sky above. There were no stars, as if they had all been eaten by the clouds. "Go on, tell me then."

"So there's this girl, right? She's driving home."

"Did they have cars in Victorian England?"

"Focus on the girl."

"How old is she?"

"Last year of college."

"Like us?"

Millie winced. "Don't interrupt."

"Just one more question."

Millie looked down at June, who was still smiling. "What?"

"Does the girl also have a girlfriend?"

"Sure, yes. She's a big old lesbian like the two of us. Can I keep going?"

June hid her smile in the padding of Millie's coat and nodded.

"So there's this girl," she started for the third time. "A lesbian girl, apparently, and she's driving home from campus."

"Our campus?" June couldn't help herself.

"Yes, our campus. She was driving home for winter break."

"I suppose it was a night just like tonight?"

"It's morning now. But a night just like last night, Christmas Eve in fact."

"Are you making this up on the spot? My brother isn't going to jump out of the bushes in a sheet or anything, is he?"

"Do you see any bushes around here?"

There were no bushes and no other likely hiding spots. They were in a small clearing, at the top of the highest hill, surrounded by the blanket of fresh snow.

"Alright, keep going."

"So, she's on the highway—you know the one. She's been driving home for a little while, trying to make it back for Christmas. Only, she's too distracted, and she's not paying attention to the road."

"What's she distracted by?"

"Her very pretty, lesbian girlfriend keeps asking her a bunch of questions in the middle of her story."

June nudged Millie's shoulder playfully, but her interest was truly piqued, so she kept her silence, and Millie got the tale back on track on her own.

"No, no. It wasn't that. The two were actually in a fight. They got in this huge, nasty fight right before the girl left, and she can't quit thinking about it."

"What were they fighting about?"

"Who can remember? The girl can't even remember. She just knows she's upset. She stormed out of the house and tossed her things in the car and got in without saying goodbye. The fight had been going for so long that she'd left later than she'd thought, and while she's driving, she realizes that it's already past midnight, and she hasn't called her parents to tell them she'll be late. They're going to be expecting her any minute, and she's still over an hour away. So she starts looking for her phone.

"Only she can't find it right away. She starts to panic a little, patting her pockets, looking around. She's wondering if she left it in the apartment, if she got it in her purse, or accidentally packed it in her luggage. She finally decides that she'll pull over and make sure her phone is in the car once she's off the highway. She's getting off at the next exit anyway. And then she hears the phone ringing."

"Is it her parents calling?"

"She doesn't know. She just hears the ringing. It's coming from under the passenger's seat. It's a small enough car, and she reaches for it, keeping one hand on the wheel, and her eyes on the road. She feels it in her fingers, still ringing, but she can't quite reach it. So she unbuckles her seat belt belt—"

"Oh no—"

"And she tries again. She reaches a little further this time, and she nearly has the phone, but she's too distracted with grabbing it to react to the patch of black ice. She's a good driver, and she does everything right from that point. She steers into the spin, she tries to get control, but her car slams into the railing, right near the overpass."

"So she died?"

"Well, her seatbelt was unbuckled. She's thrown clear. Normally the drop would have been enough to kill her, but there's this little snowdrift, from the storm. It's several feet higher than the rest of the ground, and soft, and she lands in exactly the right spot."

"Pretty lucky."

"Sort of. She's knocked unconscious. Probably concussed. But she's not bleeding too badly, and nothing's broken, so in a little while she wakes up."

"Still in the snowdrift?"

The questions were no longer coming out of habit, or to tease, June found she was genuinely engaged at this point, genuinely concerned.

"Still in the snowdrift. And she's confused. She doesn't remember the crash or know where she is. She's not thinking too clearly. The only thing she knows is that she's on her way home to her family for Christmas. She looks around and doesn't see her car or her phone or any kind of help, and so, she just decides that maybe she can walk it."

Millie fell silent then, looking out over the hill at the scenery, collecting the next part of the story. Again, June had to wonder if she was making it up on the spot, but she looked so serious.

"And?" June asked.

"Well, the next year, it's Christmas again, right?"

"Sure."

"And this girl—"

"The same girl?"

"Same girl. She's driving home from college to see her parents over the winter break. She knows the highway really well because she makes the trip a lot. It feels like second nature to her, like she may as well make this trip every day, she's super comfortable with it. Only, there are no other cars on the highway, and the snow is really coming down now, and she gets distracted. She keeps thinking back."

"To the accident?"

"No," Millie said. "To the fight."

"The ... fight?"

"Remember the fight with her girlfriend? She keeps trying to recall what they were fighting about. It must have been something really important, right? Because now she's making this trip home, alone, and she doesn't even know why. But she's angry about it still. Because it's Christmas and she shouldn't be driving so late, and alone. She knows better, and she tries to keep her eyes on the road, but she's so distracted. There's this sinking feeling in the pit of her stomach, like she knows something bad is coming. The weather is making her super nervous."

"Is it storming again?"

"Yeah, it is. But it's not like before. The snow is coming down in these big, white flakes, but it's not sticking to the ground. It looks almost like static outside the windows, and all she can see is how dark and black the road is. She knows the snow must be melting when it hits the highway but that if it freezes over, that's a recipe for black ice, which is practically invisible, and she can hardly see as is. She feels like she's been here before. She's getting so anxious. And she goes to look for her phone, only—"

"Only it's not there."

"No, no it's not. Usually it's on her person, so she keeps patting her pockets down and glancing around to the passenger's seat to her purse. She's about to give up and pull

42

over when she hears the phone ringing. Only it doesn't sound right, it doesn't sound like her phone. It sounds like—"

"Static."

Millie nodded gravely. "It sounded like static."

"And she crashes the car."

"She goes right over the railing. She wakes up in a snowdrift, just under the overpass. But she's not too injured, and she thinks maybe she can make the walk home."

"And the next year?" June asked numbly. She's pretty sure she's heard this one before.

"It's the same next year. And every year after that on Christmas. The police found her blood in the snow and tracks up to the tree line, but they never found a body. She was never put to rest. She walks until dawn, every year, just trying to make it home."

Staring up at Millie, June could see the tears rolling down her pink cheeks. She could hear the hitch in her girlfriend's breath as she tried not to cry. "She makes that walk every Christmas."

There is a tightness in June's chest as she tries to reconcile the sad story with the scenic view around her.

"Who do you think was calling?" she asks, after she's sure Millie has composed herself enough to speak.

The words are still shaky, but they come without tears. "It was the girlfriend. She wanted to apologize. It was such a stupid fight. And she can't even remember what it was about. Isn't that terrible?"

June shook her head. "It's not so terrible. It doesn't matter. The fight doesn't matter anymore."

Millie kept stroking her hair with a shaky hand until the sky showed its first signs of lightening.

"June," she whispered. "I just want to tell you that I'm—"

"Don't."

"June."

"It's okay. You don't need to say it. Please? I know. I just want to watch the sunrise with you."

So Millie held her, and the two women waited for dawn to break.

BASILE LEBRET

Basile Lebret is French and lives south of Paris.

His work has appeared in publications and translations in:
SlicedUp's Monstroddities, Atonic Vision's Strange Weeds, Bag of
Bones' Step Into the Light, Off Topic Publishing's Home, Dark Moon
Rising's The Devil's Playground, The Best of Carnage House Year
One and Underland Press' Even Cozier Cosmic & Arcana 12.

In France, in Les Feux de la Révolte by the Lufthunger Club and
soon in Malpertuis 16.

Socials
Instagram/X/Blue sky: @evoripclaw
YouTube: Vintage Book Live! does Horror
Podcast: Geoff Jones and Friends make it better

ALL IS BRIGHT

BY BASILE LEBRET

Kaïna was six when she requested a Christmas tree, and
really, this didn't bother her mother, Oumama, for she always
thought of herself as a modern woman.

Second generation Algerian, Oumama was born in
France, raised by an agnostic father and a devoted mom who
couldn't read the Qu'ran. Despite her illiteracy, Oumama's
mom, Rabbia, often claimed that the only way for her
children to rise was through education.

Those beliefs hadn't deterred Rabbia in raising Oumama as a woman, which meant a traditional wife. Oumama was the first daughter, her two older siblings were males, and this forced upon her the charge of being the eldest sister, the responsible one. Although she might never admit it, through time, Oumama had started to resent her youngest sister who she thought had it easy.

Three months before her dad passed—he had had two strokes which acted as intersignes—Oumama was planned to marry a cousin, the man her parents had chosen. Karim would become a decent father; although a family relative she didn't know, this didn't bother her. If it hadn't been her father's dying wish, Oumama would still have crumbled beneath her mother's pressure. Anywho.

Traditions made life simpler.

On her mom's behalf, she had to study first. Business management and logistics. While she was a woman of few words, Rabbia once claimed that educated women made educated guesses be it for their lives, their husbands, or their children. She had said that, with this teary throat she'd only shown at the death of her own mom, and Oumama would forever remember this scene. Her mom and her, their hands elbow deep in the couscous.

She would always remember her mom as an inhabitant of the kitchen.

The husband the family gave her, Karim, was a good man although he drank too much, albeit secretly at parties. Oumama never asked where he picked up this habit as he was raised in Algeria. He stayed gentle through the blooming of their marriage, giving her both time and space enough so she would end up trusting him. He was a loving father, did not seem to cheat on her, and did not indulge in overspending.

Oumama thought of herself as a modern woman. She had studied, didn't wear the hijab, and didn't go to the mosque. Still, she gladly partook in the Ramadan, hoped she would one day be able to make the Hajj. In her wildest dreams, she'd set enough money on the side to bring Rabbia alongside.

This was Oumama's way of walking in the footprint her mom laid in the sand when she left Kabili.

In a way, Oumama felt modern, but she also felt definitely Muslim. This forbade her to talk of the Christmas tree with her mother, who certainly would have not accepted it, and probably would have never forgiven her eldest daughter. Being Berber meant the shariah seemed both close and distant, fluent as a nearby river, and her father having defined himself as a kufr certainly didn't help. Just like Karim, her daddy had drunk, albeit less frequently, and had not prayed nor fasted through the Holy Month. As a teenager, while she resented her father for making them such a target to nay-sayers, she oftentimes admired his will in front of peer pressure. Still, Oumama's family had never celebrated Christmas, so the young mother was taken aback when Kaïna asked, "Why do all the other kids get presents, Mom?"

Despite her diplomas, Oumama's upbringing had first made her a caring mother. After having Kaïna, she landed a mediocre job in a warehouse in the suburbs of Paris, working for some GAFA whose name shall not be pronounced.

It was through her workplace that Oumama was confronted with the religious pressure her marriage had shelled her from. It seemed every day there was a good day for a young woman to pick up the veil. Or to continue fasting when the Ramadan was over. Bosses, there, could be seen exchanging in fluent Arabic, and public devotion to the religion seemed sometimes to help advancement.

She knew her colleagues would judge her if she mentioned the Christmas tree. For, if her dad had once taught her that moving to a new country certainly meant bending your back and abiding by their laws and customs, the workforce that surrounded her hadn't been raised by that man. And although Oumama sometimes felt set aside, she also had been raised by a woman who wore the shayla.

The Christmas tree felt like a treason. Not a blasphemy exactly, but once she took it home, she thought it out of place, nonetheless.

Oumama had felt the white seller's eyes judging her as she picked up the exact tree Kaïna had chosen. As if he were the one to decide what was and what was not in the right for Muslim women. "Beurette" might be the most researched word on French porn engines, and Arabs sure were allowed to fit their large bottom into tight jeans, but god forbid they ever bought a Christmas tree.

She knew some of her colleagues offered their offspring presents for Achoura—Moroccans mostly—or, as was more common, on the day of the Aïd al-Fitr. When she reflected upon it, Oumama saw this as a bending of Muslim ideology to European customs. Talking about the shariah remained a taboo topic, and French folks weren't more inclined to speak of it than Muslims. So, she kept her thoughts and her tree to herself.

The tree she had put at the end of the hallway, bordering the living room. Colleagues or not, peer pressure or tradition, she didn't dare give a more central place to what she felt was a giaour celebration, yet she still planned on adorning it with presents and decorations.

Kaïna and Oumama had a great time putting Christmas lights around the tree. She had avoided angels and Santa Claus, and everything representative really, going instead for plain golden garlands and Christmas balls. The balls were green and the lights were red and, yeah, maybe it did bother her.

Oumama had been younger once, she sometimes reminded herself. And when she was sixteen, as teens do, she had walked into a nightclub. When she closed her eyes, she could still feel the red glow which smothered them all, reminding her of the violence and the alcohol and the shots. While she felt more grounded for having done so, this night out led to no other. Yet to this day, red lights bothered her.

Karim, who at first had opposed the idea, now seemed enamored with the tree. "The blinking lights remind me of streamers. You know, like, MrBeast? We should probably install some permanent ones, once we take those off," he'd say. His breath smelled of ale and a bit of pickles.

Oumama was glad her husband had surrendered to the adventure. Or at least found a quantity of happiness that resembled her own pleasure decorating the tree with Kaïna. Yet a part of her would have preferred he'd remained

unmoved, unflinching—a face of him he exhibited scarcely—
and made her remove the tree. This would have meant
yelling, and arguments, and children being forced into
bedrooms while adults discussed. This would have also
meant turning off the Christmas lights.

In each red blink which now inhabited her living room,
Oumama saw hidden figures, dancing bodies. Hands that
gripped and did not care about consent. She could not open
up to Karim about it. Having been raised in the home country,
she was not sure he could fathom his fiancée having been into
a nightclub. In her insecure mind palace, Karim called her a
slut. But not in private. Within this distant red timeline, he
thought her a whore and cancelled the wedding under the
pretense she might not have been a virgin when she came
onto him.

All of this seemed petty and dubious. But those questions
crept on her daily. Even more so when she got home and fed
Kaïna and the lights blinked, first red, then grey, then red
again.

If anyone had asked, and if Oumama had talked, she
would have said she thought the lights coming from the tree
grew fiercer with each passing day. But this would have
meant they'd think her crazy, or worse, a munafiq.

Oumama was certain that when they had gotten the tree up, the lights stemming from the garlands had shallowly bathed the living room, faintly smeared the hall. But, in a mere week, they had crept first through the open kitchen then to the bedroom hallway.

It was Karim's idea to keep the lights blinking all through the night. And Oumama had tried pleading that she could hear it—"So you're autistic is what you're saying?"—that it wasn't good for the planet—"Since when did this household start believing in climate change?"—and then finally argued that it prevented her from sleeping—"And how can you know whether it's on or not? See, I shut it off, and you could not perceive any change." For every complaint, her husband had the answer but not the answer she wanted to hear.

Oumama did not see this as contempt or disdain. In truth, when she was at work throughout the day, she could almost see things from his perspective. Being a smart woman, she didn't know whether she was trying to smooth things out in order to keep the household stable.

A stable household meant Kaïna would be raised right. Easier than Oumama had it. She remembered expelling the tiny body from her own bloating body. The tearing she felt when she finally held her daughter, the bond too. Before Kaïna turned into a whole person with a whole personality that certainly didn't align with what Oumama had expected but was right in her own way.

And Kaïna wanted the Christmas tree, so the tree had to stay.

By then, the blinking got so strong, Oumama could perceive it through her bedroom keyhole. She thought of waking up Karim, seated in their bed. In the blue hue that was the winter night, she pondered how he could not then oppose her, could finally see what she had been perceiving for so long. The luminosity, it spread like tendrils.

Given three more days, her whole room glowed red. She thought of motels in American movies. The way those big signs always shatter the obscurity in which the hero dwells and where the enemy slithers. With every moment it turned black, she thought someone might appear. Just a silhouette, a shadow cast over the wall and getting closer.

Insomnia took hold of her brain, and bags appeared beneath her brownish eyes. Female colleagues, visibly concerned, came to ask her whether everything was okay. Had her daughter gotten sick? Was it her husband? Hijab-wearing women she'd never spoken to, inquiring about her family's health. Alhamdulillah, she just had trouble sleeping. Have you tried hot milk?

On Christmas day, the presents already layered the underbrush of the Christmas tree. Oumama did not want to open them on the 25th, thought she'd make Kaïna wait a bit. Oumama had noticed the Christmas tree had slightly slid into her living room, so she took it back to its original place.

That very same night, she could see the blinking lights through closed lids. Red. Black. Veins. Dark. She had now been awake for three days. Next to her, Karim slept on his belly, his right arm nonchalantly passed over her knees.

Unsteady, yet trying not to wake her spouse, Oumama got up. She took a pause, noticing the gentleness with whom Karim's hand settled upon the clean white sheet.

Before the whole room turned red. It felt like a visual scream. So loud it forced her to venture into the hallway, legs shaking, then the living room. Her goal still remained unclear, as she stood and instinctively faced their giant TV.

The red came back. Screaming. It was not some electric buzz she perceived within each blink. Those were voices. Indistinct, sure. Yet angry. Oumama knew she had to unplug the tree.

Within the next roaring flash, she saw them.

Through the living room glass door.

They had assembled in the cold of this Christmas night. All awake, unmoving and angry. A mob of adult males and females mostly. Arabs for the most part. The mist coming from their breath cut twirling spirals into the burning hell all around.

Darkness took over.

Red. Their mouths now distorted in angry maws, silent insults she could not perceive yet could feel. Each time the lights died off, then lit up again, there were even more. Their whispers grew louder, their breath spawned tornadoes. A single hand pressed onto the cold, cold glass. Oumama jumped, startled.

Their disappointment could now be perceived through the blackest hue.

As their number grew within the small garden, whole bodies began to press upon the window. Flesh magma, hatred, and grimaces. Oumama thought she could see the glass shatter before the night took over. She wanted to call Karim, but she didn't want to wake up Kaïna. So, when the light shut down for the last time—Oumama closed her eyes.

DON TUCKER

Don Tucker Don Tucker is a high school teacher from Massachusetts. His previous works can be found in *Doors of Darkness II: Trick or Treat* by Terrorcore Publishing and *The Daily Horrors* by Two-Headed Press.

When he is not reading or writing, he is most likely planning the next stop on his quest of attending a game at all thirty MLB stadiums.

Instagram: @don_ofthe_dead

SIX MORE WEEKS
BY DON TUCKER

The muddy banks of the Allegheny and the Pittsburgh skyline had already faded in the rearview, leaving nothing for seventeen-year-old Cassie Weber to look at besides the dreary, snow-covered landscape. She wrapped her Discman in a sweatshirt to prevent it from skipping, but her ingenuity was no match for her dad's faulty suspension. Every bump on the road sent her *Nirvana* CD thirty seconds backwards, forwards, and sometimes shut it off altogether. In her backpack were the batteries from her dad's remote control and from her little brother's remote-control car. She hoped they would power her Discman for the rest of the trip. Her family members will not be pleased when they return and find their devices powerless, but that was a problem for another day. *I'm owed that much,* she thought. *I'm being dragged through cow country on a weekend. And I'm missing the Morrison's annual Super Bowl party. My dad is getting off easy if it only costs him a handful of batteries.*

Ben, her ten-year old brother, rocked from side to side, even bumping into her, as if it would somehow help him beat the video game he was playing on his Game Boy.

"Knock it off, dipshit."

"Cassandra! Watch that language!" their dad yelled into the rearview mirror.

"Or what? You'll *turn this damn car around?* What a shame that would be!"

"Would you two stop acting like I'm torturing you? Both of you used to love this trip, remember?"

"When I was ten, maybe. I'm going to be in college in a year."

"She's just mad that she's missing the Super Bowl party," Ben chimed in.

Glenn Weber fumbled with the package on the passenger seat, trying to push a piece of nicotine gum through the thin foil. Once he bit through the thin shell and nicotine numbed his gums, he took a deep breath.

"Super Bowl? Since when do you care about football?"

"She doesn't. *Steeeeeeeve* is going to be there."

"Would you shut up, Ben?" Cassie exclaimed as she punched him in the arm.

"You two knock it off back there! And thanks for making me sit alone up here like a chauffeur, by the way."

Ben was already back to being fully engrossed in the Game Boy. Cassie heard the comment but only rolled her eyes at Glenn. They sat in silence until the tiny screen of Ben's Game Boy began to flicker. He slapped it like someone about to perform CPR.

"That's not going to help," Glenn muttered. "I'll get some batteries at the next gas station."

"*If* we see a gas station," Cassie commented while staring at snow-covered farms and fields.

60

"Cass, do you have any batteries?" Ben begged. She squeezed her backpack on the floor between her legs.

"Nope."

"Liar!"

"Keep it up back there, and I will not be buying anything!"

As the screen faded out, Ben was forced to look up and view his surroundings. It was as if he had been in his room playing with his Game Boy and he was magically transported to the back seat of his dad's station wagon. The batteries died and dropped him rudely into reality. They sat in silence, Cassie with her head on the window, imagining her crush Steve asking out Stephanie Goodwin instead of her. With the precision and concentration of a surgeon, Ben opened the back compartment of his Game Boy and rearranged the batteries and flicked the power switch on and off. Rinse and repeat.

"Do you think that's actually going to do anything? They're *dead*. And you will be too if you keep flicking that switch."

"Can we keep the death threats to a minimum please? At least until we get there," Glenn pleaded. He tucked the nicotine gum deep into his gums and found a radio station that was talking about his beloved Pirates. It was early February, just about as far away as one could get from the baseball season, but he turned it up regardless. At the moment, it took his mind off his bickering children, the wife that kicked him out of the house, and the fact that he had no cigarettes. God, he really wanted a fucking cigarette right now.

Ben, even though he was ten, still possessed the infantile quality of saying whatever popped into his head. The way a toddler might see someone at the grocery store with one arm or a rare skin disease and exclaim, *Mommy, what happened to him?*

"Dad, how long is Mom going to be mad at you?"

Glenn and Cassie made eye contact in the rearview. She rolled her eyes and resumed looking out the window. Glenn coughed into his hand.

"Um, I'm not sure, buddy. For a while. Probably."

"When can you come back home?"

"Not sure, buddy."

"Dad?"

"Yes?"

"*Why* is mom mad at you?"

"It's a long story, bud."

"Dad?"

"What is it, Ben?"

"Do you work with a bunch of cowboys and Indians or something?"

"What on earth are you talking about?"

"Like on a reservation. Where Indians live. Did you get in trouble for skipping work?"

"They're called Native Americans, idiot," Cassie snorted.

"Ben, you've been to my office. It's not an Indian reservation. What the hell are you talking about?"

"Mom had Aunt Laura over the other night. Aunt Laura said something about how you certainly weren't the first guy to get caught sneaking off the reservation. Is that why she is mad?"

Glenn and Cassie locked eyes once again in the rearview. With every fiber of her being, she tried to remain mad at him and meet him with an icy stare. She failed, and the two of them erupted in laughter while the station wagon rumbled on.

***

There were no real landmarks besides the old covered bridge they passed about ten miles ago, but Glenn knew they were almost there from the many times he took this trip. Around one of the many bends in the road, Glenn was expecting to see the "Entering Punxsutawney" sign. It was like an oasis in the middle of a desert when the kids were young, the signal to the end of a long car ride. They always laughed and pointed at the cartoon image of Punxsutawney Phil. The famous prognosticating groundhog smiled at drivers atop the sign, looking dapper in his stovepipe hat and tuxedo. That was back when the kids didn't fight so much, and they enjoyed every road trip. Back when he still shared a bed with his wife. He would trade just about anything to go back to those days.

As much as they bickered for the whole ride, Glenn smirked when he saw them fast asleep in the backseat, their heads slightly touching. Waves of nostalgia crashed into him until two small tears formed in his eyes and inched down his cheek. Suddenly they looked like toddlers to him, ecstatic to arrive at the posh Punxsutawney Inn. The staff would greet them with mugs of hot chocolate and let the kids warm up at the fireplace while the parents sorted out the checking in process. After the long ride, the kids would watch a little TV, fall asleep, and he would make love to his wife in the canopy bed while snow pelted the windows.

Reality, as it is apt to do, slowly morphs into dreams with a rude awakening. An alarm clock buzzes in the sky as you are playing mini-golf at that one place that closed twenty years ago with your elementary school gym teacher. Another dream might find you about to seal the deal with that blonde with the big tits from the grocery store, but she starts yelling "Wake up!" just as you try to take your pants off. This was no different, and the snow from his daydream began to land in big, wet drops on his windshield. Glenn turned on his wipers as the snow increased into whiteout conditions. Cassie had stirred awake, her eyes coming into focus just in time for her to yell,

"DAD! LOOK OUT!"

A majestic buck stood in the middle of the road with snow collecting on its antlers. There was no attempt to jump or flee, no fear in its eyes. Only acceptance of one's fate. He stomped the brakes to the floor, and his rusted station wagon skidded sideways. It most likely would have skidded right into the dense forest that lined the rural road if the deer hadn't blocked its path. Its torso connected with the front of the car, crumpling the hood in a groan of twisted metal as broken shards of glass from the headlights rained down, disappearing into the snow.

Glenn whipped his head around, ignoring the effects of whiplash that had already set in.

"Ben! Cass! Are you guys okay?"

They both nodded, and Glenn reached back to feel that their seatbelts were secured. He wasn't sure why. If they hadn't been buckled in, there was a good chance they would be in a mangled heap on the road in front of him. The kids groaned and rubbed their necks while an acrid smell of burnt rubber permeated the car. The dashboard hissed and dripped some sort of liquid. Still in a state of shock, they stared at the injured buck struggling to get to its feet. It succeeded for a moment, then its formidable legs failed as it collapsed in the road. They watched breath shoot from the beast's nostrils as its shaking legs allowed it to stand, probably for the last time, right before stumbling into the woods.

"Dad, is he okay?"

"Sure, buddy. Are you guys alright?"

Glenn had to kick the door open in his attempt to get out. In his frantic state of seeing if his kids were unharmed, the driveway they were at the foot of went unnoticed. Glenn wrangled his children from the car, checking them for injuries even though he didn't see any blood or broken bones. He had read somewhere that adrenaline can mask an injury, and someone in a gunfight can drop dead from a bullet they didn't even know hit them. After they insisted for the third and fourth time that they were fine, just sore, blue and red lights reflected through the storm. A patrol car pulled alongside the smoking station wagon and rolled the window down an inch or two.

"Get in!" the officer yelled over the howling storm.

"Is it going to explode?" Ben asked.

"Naw, son. You been watching too many movies. Me and your dad are going to grab anything you need from the car, though. Just in case."

The police officer opened the trunk and placed their belongings inside. The tired springs of the driver's seat sank under his heavy frame when he reentered the vehicle. He rubbed his hands in front of the blasting heaters. Glenn, sitting next to him, did the same.

"You kids staying warm back there?"

Ben and Cassie nodded.

"I'd shake your hand, but …" He tapped the cage that normally separated police from criminal.

"You don't give the bad guys much leg room," Ben observed.

"No, I suppose we don't," he chuckled. "The name's Sheriff Linsky."

"Thanks for saving our asses, Sheriff. How did you get out here so quick?"

"That would be nosy Ned, there." Sheriff Linsky nodded towards the house at the end of the driveway that Glenn had not even noticed yet. One light was on in the otherwise dark house. A curtain that was slightly pulled to the side flopped shut when Glenn glanced inside.

"You can count on Ned Oakley to report everything from teenagers driving too fast to people lighting fireworks on the Fourth of July."

"Well cheers to Ned, then."

"He's a little strange, gets under folks' skin sometimes, but he means well. So where were you folks heading? In town for the festival, I presume?"

"Yup, we never miss it."

"Old Ned there is the head of the whole festival. He's the leader of the Inner Circle. You know the guys in tuxedos that lift up the groundhog and check for the shadow? That's him."

"You don't say."

"Yup, been doing it for years. I can give you a lift into town, though. The tow truck is already on its way. Where's your room at?"

"The Punxsutawney Inn," said Cassie from the back seat.

"Actually, we are at the Gobbler's Knob Motor Lodge," corrected Glenn.

"What?" the kids replied in unison.

Glenn spun his head around and spoke to his children through his teeth.

"The Punxsutawney Inn was easier to swing when me and your mother were splitting it. This year, we are at the Gobbler's Knob Motor Lodge."

"This trip keeps getting better and better," Cassie moaned.

Not wanting to get involved in a familial spat, Sheriff Linsky interjected, "There is one piece of business that I need to straighten out before the tow gets here. Law says I need to check whether or not Bambi is actually, uh, expired."

"And if it isn't?" Cassie asked.

"Well young lady, I would have to put it out of its misery."

"You would shoot it?"

"Yes ma'am. It's the humane thing to do. It's all yours if you want it, too. We got someone in town that could clean and butcher it for you. You could brag to all your friends that you bagged a ten-pointer."

"Thanks Sheriff, but I think we will pass."

The increasing storm had all but covered the dying animal's tracks into the woods. Sheriff Linsky told the Webers to hang tight, and he exited the vehicle and zipped up his parka to his nose. Just as he was turning on his flashlight, no more than ten paces into the trees, he spotted the animal in a mangled mess. Breath dwindled from its nostrils and dissipated in the beam of the flashlight in faint strands. Sheriff Linsky made the sign of the cross, drew his pistol, and fired one shot between its soulful eyes. The labored breaths of the buck ceased, and a thin tributary of blood colored the snow red. Inside the car, Cassie and Ben Weber covered their ears and wept. The Sheriff entered the car in silence and yanked the shifter into drive. Two beady eyes followed the vehicle as it sputtered along the lonely road. A small creature, no more than two feet tall, stood on a tree stump and watched patiently as Sheriff Linsky's car crested over a hill and out of sight. Glenn sat in the passenger seat and wondered where his life went wrong.

***

Glenn had set the alarm clock in the room for 8:00, but he awoke long before that was a factor. He certainly thought he was going to sleep in after the night's events but perhaps the smell of the dingy room awoke him sooner. The tacky wallpaper and outdated curtains practically dripped with nicotine. Before they passed out, the kids complained about the stench, but Glenn salivated at the clean, glass ashtray that sat on the end table. He wanted nothing more than to watch a bad movie in his underwear, alone, with the ashtray resting on his belly while the thick curtains blotted out reality.

The sun was just inching over the horizon, and the coffee that he saw in the metal urn when he checked in suddenly sounded like a fantastic idea, regardless if it was the same pot from the night before. No one was at the front desk when he filled a Styrofoam cup with the brown sludge. There was no sugar or cream laying around, but he accepted it as a beggars-cannot-be-choosers scenario. The snow had stopped, and the plows had yet to make their rounds, leaving everything in an untouched white blanket. He blew on his coffee and patted his breast pocket out of muscle memory for the cigarettes that did not exist and sighed.

At the end of the long row of rooms sat two glowing vending machines. Glenn zipped up his jacket and walked past the rooms that still had their curtains drawn tight. Cheap plastic furniture covered in snow sat on the concrete walkway outside the rooms. At the Punxsutawney Inn, Glenn pictured the families arriving in the dining room for a magnificent spread of thick slab bacon, omelets, fresh-baked muffins, and their signature crème brûlée french toast. This year, his kids would have to settle for some halfway-frozen snacks from a vending machine.

Directly next to the machines stood a cylindrical metal ashtray. A single cigarette rested in the grooves on the sides. Next to it sat a book of matches. Glenn reasoned that it could not have been there long; the wind certainly would have blown it away. Upon closer inspection, the cigarette was unlit and stamped on the paper right by the filter read "Camel." His former brand. Glenn backed up a few steps so he could see his room on the second floor, no lights or TV on yet. Definitely asleep.

The cigarette felt familiar in his hand. The mere smell of the tobacco comforted him. His soon-to-be-ex-wife and children had begged him for years to quit, and when he sat at the precipice of losing his entire family, he decided to give them up for good. Until now. If he lit it where he stood, the smell would certainly waft up towards his room. The cigarette danced in his lips as he meandered behind the building. The first match popped and went out instantly. The second one held a flame but went out as he moved it towards his lips. The third match went out instantly. Only four matches remained in the book as Glenn Weber contemplated his options. He could honor the promise he made to his family, and to himself, and simply walk away. While he was considering those options, he ripped the four matches free, held them in a bunch, and popped them against the strip. It would either work, or they would all go out. A go-big-or-go-home situation. It worked long enough to light the cigarette. Glenn groaned with an almost sexual level of satisfaction and leaned his head on the bricks of the building. Only mere inches from where he stood, an avalanche of snow rained down from the roof.

"Son of a bitch!"

"You alright down there? Sorry, I didn't see anyone down there. There's not usually any guests back here on February 1st at 5:30 in the morning. You lost?" the man shouted from the roof.

"I quit smoking," he shouted back while holding up the lit cigarette for him to see.

"I've been there before. You checked in yesterday with those two kids, right? I'll knock $25 off your bill if you help me shovel the rest of this. Not too much left."

"You had me at $25 off," Glenn remarked as he ascended the rickety metal staircase that led to the second-floor roof of the motel.

"Don't worry! She don't look sturdy, but she'll hold," the man shouted.

Glenn got to the roof where the man from the front desk already had his hand extended.

"Not sure if I introduced myself last night but the name's Hank Summerbell."

"Supperbell?"

"Summer. Like the season. Wish I could say I made it up, but that's the name the good lord gave me."

"Well, nice to meet you, Hank. Got an extra one of those shovels?"

"Sure do, right over here."

It wasn't until Hank shuffled over to grab the roof shovel that Glenn noticed he had a severe limp.

"Whoever built this place," Hank commented as he pushed a pile of snow off the roof, "must have thought he was in Florida. Who the hell builds a flat roof this long in Pennsylvania?"

"That's a fair point."

"Now don't go taking a header off the roof and suing the pants off me," Hank laughed.

"I wasn't planning on it. But now that you mention it …"

A few moments went by and Hank asked, "Hey you alright over there?"

Glenn stood at the edge of the roof after pushing off a pile, staring at the field behind the motel. He stood frozen, and not just from the temperature. In the field, clear as day, were the words "SMOKING KILLS." It was spelled big enough to be seen by a low-flying plane, like a message from someone on a deserted island. The sun from the untouched white landscape blinded him, and the wind howled, but his eyes eventually determined what the letters were composed of. Arms, legs, heads, and torsos arranged with surgical precision. A pile of heads functioned as the dot on the "I." Fully intact corpses, slightly bent with fingertips touching the toes of the person above it formed the "O." Whatever created this ran out of bodies, and the "S" in *KILLS* was made entirely from spools of intestine. Just under the words was the stump of an oak tree. The stump and the surrounding snow were stained with so much blood they looked black. A groundhog, no more than two feet tall, stood on the stump eating a human leg like corn on the cob. Bits of flesh and blood sprayed in all directions as it rotated the limb. Seemingly satisfied, it dropped the leg with a thump into the snow and looked up, making direct eye contact with Glenn. The small creature's mouth opened with a blood-drenched smile.

"Hey! You alright over there?" Hank asked, grabbing his shoulder and pulling him back from the roof's edge. When Glenn looked back, the message was gone. Just another field covered in snow.

"Yes. Ya. Uh, just thought I saw something out there."

"Thought you were about to take that header after all."

"Thanks. I guess I didn't realize how close I was getting."

"No problem. I 'preciate the help and all. Don't get around like I used to," Hank said as he tapped the shovel against his shin with a metallic *ting*. He reached down and pulled up his snow pants a few inches to reveal a metal prosthetic leg. Glenn's stomach shuddered as he imagined the missing part of his leg being gnawed to the bone.

"Happy to help."

***

Glenn and Ben were showered and ready. It took a bit of convincing for Cassie to step foot into the mildew-ridden shower, but once she was ready, they bundled up and walked towards the festivities in the center of town.

"Dad?" Ben asked as they walked along the busy sidewalks.

"Yes?"

"Shouldn't we tell Mom about the car?"

"You know how Mom is," Cassie said. "She'll just freak out. Nothing we can do about it now."

"Cassie's right. No need to worry your mother. Hopefully they can fix the car before we leave, and everything will be as good as new."

It was February 1st, the day before Groundhog Day, and Punxsutawney was electric and bustling with activities. The small town's population nearly tripled for the days surrounding February 2nd, as people participated in face-painting, live music, and pierogi eating contests. On this morning, the Weber family were on their way to the annual pancake and sausage breakfast hosted by the Inner Circle. They were a group of men nearly as old as the holiday itself, adorned in tuxedos and stovepipe hats, that planned and oversaw all events relating to the world's most famous weather-predicting groundhog.

The Punxsutawney Community Center was filled, as were their stomachs, when the members of the Inner Circle took the stage. Glenn recognized Ned, the man he saw briefly from behind his living room curtains.

"Hear ye, hear ye," Ned bellowed. "The official Punxsutawney Groundhog Club would like to extend our warmest welcome, and we certainly hope that you all enjoyed this lovely breakfast. Whether you have lived in Punxsutawney all your life, or you're a first-time visitor, welcome! I will save the longer speech for tomorrow, bright and early at Gobbler's Knob. But for now, we will kick off the Groundhog Parade, so let's bring out the man of the hour. Kids, we are going to need your help. He can be a little shy, so let's start a *PHIL* chant. *PHIL! PHIL! PHIL! PHIL!*"

The room shook as every man, woman, and child chanted his name and stomped their feet. Finally, to raucous applause, Punxsutawney Phil emerged on the stage. Only it was a man in a bizarre groundhog costume, wearing the official tuxedo and stovepipe hat garb.

"That's not the *real* Punxsutawney Phil," groaned Ben.

"No shit, Sherlock," Cassie retorted.

"Don't be a smartass. You are correct, Ben. That is not the real Phil, but he is wearing Phil's actual hat."

Ben made a face, sticking out his tongue at Cassie once Glenn turned away.

The Inner Circle rolled out a red carpet all the way to the exit and marched behind their town mascot.

"Dad, are you okay? You're white as a ghost."

"Yes, I'm fine," he snapped.

"Geez, just asking."

Only Glenn Weber was not fine. While children cheered at the jovial looking groundhog, Glenn saw something that no one else did. It was the face of the groundhog in the field, dripping blood from its bucktoothed smile, winking at Glenn as he passed. Glenn squeezed the hands of his children when Phil stopped and turned to face him:

"You drive into town and kill my friends?

Punxsutawney is where your life will end.

Screwing your secretary, what a walking cliché!

I will make your life end today.

You had it all, what did you think?

Will that be the last time you dip your pen in the company ink?"

"Dad!" Ben and Cassie shouted in unison as he squeezed their hands so hard they felt like they would pop. They shouted loud enough to draw some concerned looks.

"Sorry, I guess I spaced out for a second."

At Ben's insistence, the Webers followed the group outside in order to get a good spot to watch the parade. The sidewalks were lined with cheering people as members of the Inner Circle, and the Phil impostor entered a convertible with the top down, which seemed comical in the bitter cold. They found a spot about a block down from the community center where they squeezed in between two families.

Glenn got a much better look at Ned this time around. There were four members of the Inner Circle in the vehicle, two up front and two in the back with Phil sandwiched in the middle. The car seemed to inch along in slow motion, giving Glenn enough time to notice some sort of malady on each member of the Inner Circle. Peeking out from a winter coat was a gauze-covered arm. Another rider had some sort of bandage on his ear. Ned, who was waving from the passenger seat, had a small bandage on his neck. The groundhog half-stood in the back seat, pointing a tube towards the sky, and pulled a string. Confetti flew in the air as a gust of wind ripped through Main Street, taking the groundhog's hat and sending it to Cassie's feet. Spectators were too busy watching the confetti cannon to spot where the hat ended up. She scanned her surroundings briefly, punched the top of the hat to flatten it, and stuffed it in her oversized winter coat. For a brief moment, Cassie thought she saw the groundhog's head spin around and smile at her with blood dripping from its teeth.

***

They returned to the Gobbler's Knob Motor Lodge exhausted, opting to not go to the annual Groundhog Banquet at Town Hall. The kids were frozen stiff and begged Glenn to get a pizza and bring it back to the room instead. Glenn fell asleep half-sitting up in his bed, forcing Cassie to blare the volume on the TV once the snoring set in. It was an ancient behemoth of a TV, and Cassie fiddled with the rabbit ear antennae hoping to pick up MTV. The only two stations she could get were a local public access station broadcasting some sort of mind numbingly boring town meeting and reruns of *I Love Lucy*. She settled for *I Love Lucy*. It was the classic episode where Lucy and Ethel find themselves at the chocolate factory. They quickly become overwhelmed with the speed of the conveyor belt, forcing them to shove chocolates into their mouths. Cassie smiled as she remembered how much her grandmother loved this episode. They start with such confidence, wrapping the chocolates by hand with ease. The conveyor belt increases, and hilarity ensues. The belt suddenly froze on the TV, along with Lucy and Ethel. Assuming it was a reception issue, Cassie stood up to once again jiggle the rabbit ears. Right before her hand could reach it, the conveyor belt on the screen resumed humming at a high speed.

"What the hell?" Cassie whispered.

The chocolates on the belt continued to whir by the screen, but Lucy and Ethel remained frozen. The belt increased to hyper speed, sending the chocolates flying. The belt came to a screeching halt, and in the dead center of the screen sat good old Punxsutawney Phil.

"Give. It. Back. GIVE IT BACK!"

Phil's tiny paw emerged through the screen and pointed at his crumpled hat in the corner of the room.

"Give it back.

Cover your mouth and stifle those shrieks.

If I see my shadow, you'll only have six more weeks.

Six more weeks!

Six more weeks!

Six more weeks!"

Cassie reached for the dial and shut off the TV just before Phil's bloody paw could reach her. She tiptoed around her sleeping father and brother before she bundled up, grabbed the hat, and ventured into the frigid night towards Gobbler's Knob. It was past midnight, and the only light that was on was the one that said "OFFICE" and "NO VACANCY." The door to the office was wide open, and a thin trail of blood led through the parking lot. She sprinted towards Gobbler's Knob until her throat burned, falling twice in the slushy snow. Eventually she reached the clearing and the grandiose sign that read "Welcome to Gobbler's Knob."

In just a few short hours, this desolate area would be overflowing with people and camera crews documenting the annual affair. Front and center sat the famous tree stump. At the break of dawn, the Inner Circle would march out and rap on the tiny door with a wooden cane. The crowd would fall silent as they reach into the stump and pull out the prognosticator of prognosticators for the big reveal, groans for six more weeks of winter or cheers for an early spring. Cassie ducked behind a bush as she heard hushed whispers and feet crunching on snow. Out of the shadows emerged roughly ten men, all in matching tuxedos and top hats. The Inner Circle. They walked out in single file, then dispersed into a semi-circle, facing the stump. The last man in line was Ned Oakley, their leader. He exited the shadows backwards, dragging a corpse through the snow and leaving it just in front of the tree stump.

The corpse was not a corpse after all; it slowly began to writhe and groan in the snow. Cassie saw the faint twinkle of a metal prosthetic leg as he struggled.

"If Mary's purifying day,

be clear and bright with sunny ray,

the frost and cold shall be much more,

after the feast than was before."

Their voices echoed into the night as they repeated the verse. They echoed the verse five times and then began to repeat the last line:

"After the feast than was before."

"After the feast than was before."

Ned rapped on the door with the cane. Some rustling could be heard within the stump, and it creaked open. The lovable Punxsutawney Phil crawled around the body, sniffing every inch. It seemed to be normal behavior from the woodland creature until it leaped onto the man's stomach. It stood on its hind legs, exposed its long buck teeth, and buried them into the man's stomach, sinking through the flesh. The adorable and friendly Phil sank his entire head into Hank's stomach and emerged with intestines hanging from his mouth. Hank Summerbell sent a blood-curdling scream into the night with the last of his energy. It was no use; Phil had already begun to scale a tree with a death grip on Hank's unravelling guts. With one quick shake of his head, he twirled the innards until they wrapped around Hank's neck and around a tree branch. Hank Summerbell swung from the macabre noose, and each time his momentum swung him into the tree, his prosthetic leg clanked against the rough bark.

Cassie was doing her best to stay undetected, but the sheer terror and freezing temperatures rushing through her shook the bush.

"GIVE IT BACK! GIVE IT BACK! WHAT ARE YOU WAITING FOR? GET HER!"

In unison, the Inner Circle gave chase to Cassie who sprinted down the middle of the street. All she could hear were their dress shoes slapping against the pavement, growing nearer. Ned got close enough to swing out his wooden cane and take out Cassie at the knees.

"Just take the fucking hat! I don't want it!"

Ned straddled Cassie in the middle of the street. He only smiled, and raised his wooden cane straight into the air, ready to plunge it through her heart. Before he could do so, a car came barreling down the street, blinding Ned with its spotlight. Sheriff Linsky scrambled from his patrol car and yelled. "Freeze!"

"Evening Sheriff," Ned muttered as he drove the cane downward. The cane never touched her. Linsky emptied his revolver into his chest and Ned fell to the ground with a thud.

"You alright?"

"Ya, I think so," Cassie stammered.

"Then get in!"

Cassie climbed into the back seat, scanning her surroundings. Sheriff Linsky waited for additional officers to arrive at the scene before taking Cassie back to her family. There were no signs of the Inner Circle or Phil as Sheriff Linsky's cruiser began to navigate the icy roads.

***

Once Glenn got his car back and pleaded with the garage owner to not cash his check until next Thursday, they drove home mostly in silence. Cassie sat up front this time, and once Ben dozed off in the backseat, they spoke about what they saw. They both wanted to deny it, but there was no denying the look on her father's face when he nearly squeezed her hand into bone broth. Since then, it mostly hung between them like a dark cloud. Life returned to normal, as much as it could, after what the media dubbed as the "Groundhog Day Massacre." There were no reports of human sacrifices or talking groundhogs. Hank Summerbell's death was painted as the deranged acts of a lone psychopath.

"Dad?" she said one Saturday evening back in the Pittsburgh suburbs.

"Ya, Cass?"

Glenn was preoccupied with preparing a traditional Saint Patrick's Day feast. Cabbage, corned beef, potatoes. Ben and Cassie always complained, reminding their father that they were not Irish and that it smelled like feet.

"It's Saint Patrick's Day, Dad," Cassie commented.

"How did you figure that out?" he replied sarcastically in his green sweater that said, "KISS ME I'M IRISH."

"Well, if you look at a calendar … Groundhog Day was just about six weeks ago."

They exchanged a glance in silence, not wanting to alarm Ben. He was once again engrossed in his Game Boy and did not hear the comment. Glenn approached her and got on one knee as he placed his hands on her shoulders.

"It's over, Cass. It's all over. Remember what Dr. Gallen has been teaching you. That man, I don't even want to say his name, he can't hurt you. Remember, you saw Sheriff Linsky kill him. He's dead, in the ground, forever."

"It's not just him, Dad."

He removed his hands from her shoulders and resumed fiddling with the steaming pot of corned beef and cabbage. She followed him into the kitchen.

"Dad, I know we only talked about it once. But you told me what you saw. You *know* that it was real."

"Keep. Your. Voice. Down," Glenn said through his teeth, glancing at Ben in the living room.

"Goddammit Dad! Stop acting like it never happened! It has been six weeks, I know you have been looking at the calendar just as much as I have!"

"Why are you guys yelling?" Ben asked over the beeping device.

"Nothing, buddy! Cass taste-tested dinner for me, and she said it is extra feet-like this year."

He immediately shifted his happy-go-lucky tone that he was using for Ben's sake into a stern whisper.

"What do you think is going to happen, Cass? A rodent is going to hitchhike two hours down Route 28 and eat us?"

"Is it anymore crazy then what has already happened?"

"It's over Cassandra. It's all over," Glenn said as he brought her in close and hugged her closer than he ever had.

"Ya. You're probably right."

"Now, can we please have a nice evening?"

Cassie nodded.

The oven dinged.

"Is that the soda bread?" Ben asked hopefully.

"Sure is, buddy! Come and get it while it's hot!"

What could not be heard over the traditional Irish music that was blasting on the stereo was a small rodent, no more than two feet tall, chewing its way through their back door.

 DM PELLEY

DM Pelley is a former medical entomologist who started writing short horror pieces in the 1980's. His books include "The Horror I Saw," "Goat Roper," and "The Beast of Orange Blossom Trail."

Fun fact: Pelley wrote the screenplay for the movie Super Death Kill (which he also directed), along with a handful of spec scripts that mostly freaked out the entertainment industry.

Raised in Colorado, Pelley "believes in UFOs, astral projections, mental telepathy, ESP, clairvoyance, spirit photography, telekinetic movement, full trance mediums, the Loch Ness monster, and the theory of Atlantis."

Author Website: <u>DM Pelley</u>
Instagram: <u>@d_m_pelley</u>

SANTA EATS MEAT
BY DM PELLEY

Frank Schmeck's pickup truck rumbled along the snow-dusted highway, its headlights cutting through the swirling flakes. Christmas Eve had crept up, and the vast, empty stretch of Route 17 felt like the edge of the world. Frank was exhausted, his eyes bleary from days of driving cross-country, chasing a fresh start after a year that had chewed him up and spit him out. The radio crackled with faint strains of *Silent Night, Holy Night*, but he switched it off, preferring the engine's hum and the whisper of snow flattening under the tires. He was alone, as he'd been for years. But tonight, the loneliness stung a little sharper.

Ahead, a sign flickered in the glow of his headlights: Frostwick, 5 Miles. Frank had found the town online, a speck on the map, and booked a cabin rental to get off the road for Christmas Eve. He'd never heard of Frostwick, but the website promised a "charming winter retreat," and the price was right. As he turned onto the exit, the road narrowed, flanked by towering pines heavy with snow.

The town emerged like a postcard: cottages aglow with strings of colored lights, their reflections dancing in the icy sheen of a frozen creek. A church steeple pierced the cloudy sky, its bell tolling softly, and the faint laughter of children echoed from somewhere unseen. Snow fell in gentle veils, softening the world into something almost magical.

Frank's chest loosened, a faint smile tugging at the corners of his mouth. Frostwick was quaint, alive with the kind of Christmas spirit he'd thought existed only in old movies. For a moment, he felt a flicker of warmth, a reminder of childhood winters when the holiday meant more than just another day.

He followed the GPS to a winding lane on the town's outskirts, where a weathered cabin waited, its roof blanketed in snow. The porch light glowed with amber warmth, casting a golden pool over a stack of firewood and a plastic wreath. Frank parked, grabbed his duffel bag, and stepped into the crisp air, the snow crunching under his boots. The scent of pine and woodsmoke filled his lungs, and he let out a long breath. Maybe this stop would do him some good.

Inside, the cabin was cozy, if a bit dated. A sagging couch faced a stone fireplace, and a small kitchen held a fridge stocked with basics: milk, eggs, a couple of steaks. A string of Christmas lights blinked along the windows, their colors painting the walls in soft reds and greens. Frank tossed his bag onto the couch, too tired to unpack. The clock on the wall read eight p.m. He considered a shower but opted for sleep, trudging to the bedroom and collapsing onto the flannel-sheeted bed. The cabin creaked as it settled, the wind outside a low lullaby. Frank's eyes drifted shut, the charm of Frostwick lingering in his mind as he fell into a deep sleep.

Hours (or minutes) later, a wet, tearing crunch snapped him awake. His eyes flew open, heart pounding as he lay still, straining to hear. The cabin was dark, the Christmas lights casting faint, eerie shadows. The clock ticked just past midnight, and the air was colder now, laced with a sour, rotting stench that made his stomach twist. Another crunch came, followed by a low, guttural murmuring sound as if someone nearby were talking to themself. The sound was close, and as he tilted his head toward the noise, he realized with horror that it was coming from the kitchen.

Frank sat bolt upright, his breath clouding in the frigid air. He'd locked the door, hadn't he? His mind raced, conjuring images of a drifter or worse. He quickly reached for his phone and realized with growing panic that he had left it on the center console of his car. Frank took a deep breath and knew he was on his own.

He stealthily slipped out of bed and crept towards the door, hoping he would hear the sounds of someone leaving out the door or noisily climbing out a window. Instead, the sounds grew more ravenous and guttural, as if someone was eating a sloppy barbecue sandwich with gusto. Frank looked around the room for something, anything, that he could use as a weapon. The room was rather plain, and his only hope lie in the closet which he hadn't even bothered to open when he first came in. Frank padded over to the door and opened it as quietly as he could. There was a faint "squeak" which caused him to grimace, but he managed to get it open enough so that he could reach in and feel around. At first, his groping hand felt nothing, but then he encountered something leaning against the corner, and he involuntarily smiled.

A baseball bat. He pulled it out and grasped it with two hands, and its weight steadied him. He crept back towards the bedroom door and paused to listen.

The muttering grew louder, punctuated by the clatter of dishes. The stench hit him harder, like spoiled meat festering in a summer dumpster. Frank's grip tightened on the bat as he edged down the short hallway, the Christmas lights flickering as if in warning.

He rounded the corner into the kitchen and froze, his blood turning to ice. There, hunched in front of the open fridge, was Santa Claus.

This was not the kindly old man that he had grown up seeing on TV and postcards. This Santa was a grotesque mockery of St. Nick, clad in a tattered red suit, the white trim stained with dark, crusty smears. Its hat hung crooked, revealing a scalp of patchy gray hair clinging to a skull that gleamed wetly in the fridge's light. The face was a nightmare: skin sagging like melted wax, one eye a milky void, the other glowing a sickly yellow. Its mouth worked furiously, tearing into a raw steak from the fridge, blood and juices dripping down its matted beard. It paused, sensing Frank, and turned slowly. The glowing eye fixed on him, and its lips peeled back to reveal jagged, crimson-stained teeth.

"Santa eats meat!" it said with a gurgling sound, the voice merely air forced through rotted airways and a corpse's lips.

Frank's scream caught in his throat. Inexplicably, instinct kicked in, and he swung the bat, aiming for the creature's head, but it moved with unnatural speed, catching the bat in a gnarled, claw-like hand. The wood splintered under its grip, and Frank stumbled back, crashing into the kitchen table.

Zombie Santa lurched forward, dropping the steak with a wet slap. Its sleigh bells, rusted and dangling from the coat, jingled discordantly with each step. "Santa eats meat."

Frank scrambled to his feet, grabbing a butcher knife from the counter. "Stay back!" he shouted, but the creature only grinned, its chant unrelenting. "Santa eats meat!"

The knife slashed across Santa's chest, tearing the rotten fabric and sinking into gray flesh. Black ichor oozed from the wound, but the monster barely flinched. It swiped at Frank, its claws raking his arm. Pain seared through him, blood welling through his torn sleeve. Frank stabbed again, aiming for the neck, but Santa's hand shot out, seizing his wrist. The strength was crushing, bones grinding as Frank gasped. With a desperate twist, he broke free, diving for the living room.

The cabin shook as Santa pursued, its heavy steps splintering the floorboards. Frank's eyes darted wildly, landing on the fireplace poker. He grabbed it, spinning just as Santa lunged. The poker drove into the zombie's neck, pinning it momentarily to the wall. Frank didn't wait, and he bolted for the stairs, his only thought to reach the attic to buy some time. The poker tore free with a sickening squelch, and Santa's chant followed, louder, and even more hungry. "Santa eats meat!"

Frank reached the attic, slamming the trapdoor shut and dragging a heavy trunk over it. His arm throbbed, blood dripping onto the dusty floor. The attic was cramped, filled with old boxes and a single, frost-covered window. Outside, the snow fell harder, the serene beauty of Frostwick now a cruel contrast to the horror below. The trapdoor bucked as Santa pounded it, wood splintering. With each strike Santa's corpse bellowed, "Santa eats meat!"

Frank's heart raced. He couldn't stay in the attic forever. Frank knew the roof was his only chance.

He smashed the window with a box, the glass shattering into the snow below. The cold bit at his wounds as he climbed out, the slanted wood slick under his bare feet. He clambered onto the roof, his chest heaving from the effort. The night was no longer silent or holy; the wind howled, carrying the faint snarls of something damned and reanimated below him.

Before he could think, Frank's breath stopped as he saw them. Zombie reindeer, their skeletal forms lurching through the snow around the cabin. Their antlers were jagged, their fur patchy and matted with gore. Their eyes glowed the same yellow as Santa's, and their mouths snapped open, revealing rotted, huge buckteeth. They sensed him, their heads snapping upward, and they began to jerkily circle the cabin like a pack of rabid wolves.

Frank heard the trapdoor explode inside the attic, and a moment later, Santa peered over the edge of the roof at him, its face twisted into a rictus of hunger. "Santa eats meat!" it roared, crawling onto the roof with terrifying speed.

Frank backed away, his heels brushing the roof's edge. The reindeer snorted below, their snarls mixing with the jingling of Santa's bells into a nightmarish cacophony. Frank had no weapons, no plan, only the primal urge to survive.

Santa charged, its claws raised in anticipation. Frank ducked, slipping on the icy shingles, and tackled the creature's legs. They crashed together, sliding toward the roof's edge. Santa's claws tore into Frank's back, shredding skin and muscle. Blood soaked his shirt, but Frank screamed in anger, fueled by pain and desperation. He drove his elbow into Santa's face, feeling the rotten nose smush like an over baked potato. The creature howled, momentarily stunned, and

Frank scrambled free, seizing a large, broken, wooden shingle as a makeshift blade.

Santa roared and flew at Frank, and the two of them flew off the roof in a tangle of limbs and landed in the snow below with a loud crunch. Frank flipped Santa off and rolled onto his side, wiping blood from the corner of his mouth.

Just then, the reindeer attacked, the first one lunging for his throat. Frank swung the shingle, and to his surprise half of the animal's rotted face went flying off into the dark. Black blood sprayed, and the beast recoiled, but another took its place, its antlers goring Frank's thigh. He screamed, falling to his knees, but slashed again, severing the reindeer's neck to the bone.

The creatures circled, relentless, their glowing eyes unblinking. Santa rose, its chest heaving, and joined the assault, its claws aimed at Frank's heart. "Santa eats meat!"

Frank rolled, the claws grazing his chest, and gripped his roof tile like the hilt of a knife. He hurled it, piercing Santa's soggy, milky eye. The creature staggered, and Frank seized the moment, leaping onto its back. He wrapped his arm around its neck, squeezing with all his strength. Santa thrashed, its bells jingling wildly, but Frank held on, his vision blurring from blood loss. The reindeer closed in, their

100

teeth snapping. Frank kicked one away, and its skull cracked against the chimney.

Santa's claws dug into Frank's arm, peeling flesh, but Frank tightened his grip, feeling the creature's neck bones grind. "Santa … eats … meat …" it strained, as it turned to bite Frank.

With a primal scream, Frank twisted, severing Santa's spine as he ripped the zombie's head off like a rotted pumpkin and flung it into the woods. The zombie's body went limp, its chant finally silenced. Frank shoved the body off himself and watched as black fluid pooled around its still twitching body.

The reindeer paused, their movements faltering without their master. Frank didn't hesitate. He grabbed a big fallen pine branch and used it like a sword, slashing and stabbing, his hands slick with blood and black goo. One reindeer fell, its front legs cut off. Another gored his side, but Frank drove the branch into its eye, twisting until it collapsed. The last beast charged, and Frank met it head-on, tackling it like a pro wrestler. They slid into a snowbank with the force of a runaway locomotive. Frank's vision swam, but he grabbed an antler and twisted, breaking it off. With his last bit of strength, he plunged it back into the reindeer's skull, again and again, until it stopped moving.

He lay there, gasping, the snow soaking red beneath him. The night was silent once more, the storm easing, the stars peeking through thinning clouds. Frostwick's lights twinkled in the distance, oblivious to the carnage. Frank's body screamed with pain, his wounds gaping, but he was alive. He crawled back to the cabin, collapsing by the fireplace. The Christmas lights still glowed, their festiveness lost after the scene outside.

As dawn broke, Frank bandaged his wounds with torn sheets, his hands trembling. He burned Santa's remains and the reindeer carcasses, the fire roaring until nothing remained but ash.

Christmas Day had arrived, quiet and cold. Frank sat by the window, a mug of whiskey in his hand, watching the snow fall. The town would celebrate, singing carols, unwrapping gifts, and exchanging tidings—and Frank would let them do so in peace, his gift to them.

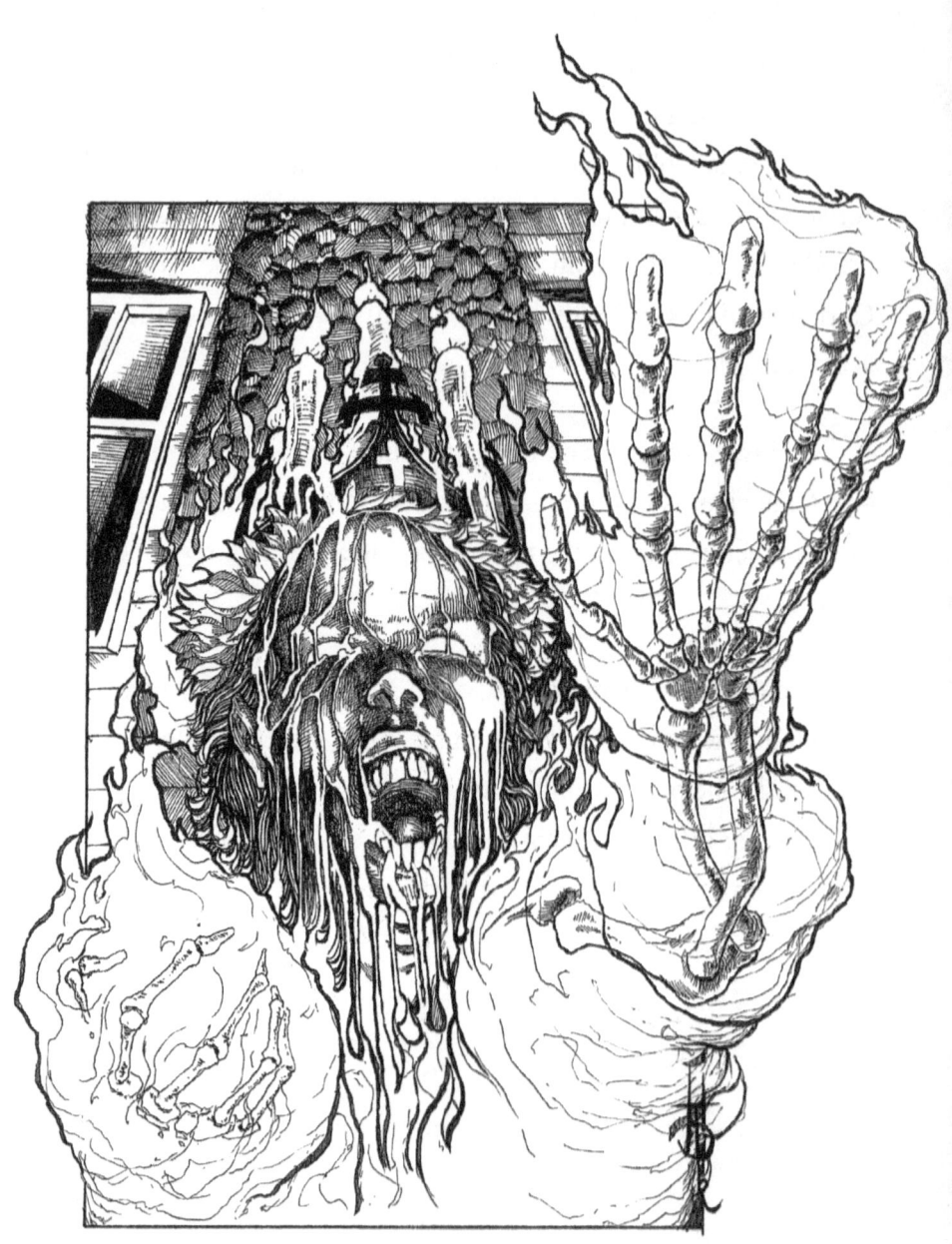

DESIREE HORTON

Desiree Horton is a horror writer and enthusiast. She can be found at home in the PNW with her two dogs, two kids, and one husband.

Her work can be found in other horror anthologies, and on the edges of papers she will lose almost immediately. Her other full length works include Midnight Mother, Of Teeth and Pine, and What Comes From Between, and can be found wherever books are sold.

More information on her works can be found at authordesireehorton.my.canva.site or on Amazon.
Instagram and tiktok: @horrortonwritesabook

LUCY BRINGS THE LIGHT
BY DESIREE HORTON

I am awakened by a voice that I can feel in my bones. It feels warm, like holding your hands over a fire after playing in the snow. The voice begins to whisper inside my skull, a sound like boulders falling into the sea.

"It's your feast day today," it says, "the feast of Santa Lucia."

I have heard the voice of the angel before, the sound of storms, wind, and rain, but this time is different. This time, it tells me of the blessed holiday and bestows upon me two most precious gifts. One is pressed right into my hand as I lie in the dark, listening to the dim cacophony of people in the house above me, talking, laughing, and chatting. The angel's holy touch burns ice cold on the scraps still left of my flesh like a stinging balm–the other gift, a holy miracle.

I know winter is here. The ground I sleep upon is cold and hardened. I used to cry. I used to wish I could make them hear me down here beneath the house, to get them to set me free.

"Listen to me, please! My name is Lucy!" I would scream. "Please let me out of here! I can't see!"

No one heard me, or at least, no one answered. The old man who put me down here has not been back for a long, long time. I think he may be dead. But somehow, I'm not. I'm still here, lost and cold, unable to find my way out.

The old man put my eyes out long ago with the fire poker. It was fresh from the fire, so the heat would cauterize the wounds. He didn't want me to die, but he wanted to make sure I couldn't solve his labyrinth in the depths of the basement, in the spaces between walls where he imprisoned me. I used to wish for my eyes.

I stopped wishing.

I stopped hoping.

Until today.

The angel came down to tell me it's Santa Lucia's feast day. *My* day. It presses its fiery hand upon my face, and when it's gone, I'm changed. I am whole again. My eyes are once more round in their sockets, spying the glow through the cracks in the walls. A miracle. It's strange to see this place for the first time, the wood and plaster, insulation and insect nests, all these things that had been with me all along.

To feel the dampness and shape of eyes within my long-empty sockets is thrilling. I begin to weep, enjoying the succulence upon my delicate, decomposing flesh. The salt from my tears burns the places where the epidermis has worn away from what lies beneath. Sweet suffering.

As my newfound eyes grow accustomed to the dark, I see a hint of light ahead of the place where my head has rested these many years. I live, yet I decay, and now, filled with the light of God and the gift of sight, I yearn to feel the warmth of love once more, the warmth of family, laughter, and good cheer, to taste the saffron buns and sweet, warm glögg. I hear the muffled sound of a phone ringing somewhere above me. Someone answers.

"Hello? Lucille! Yes, darling, that's wonderful! I can't wait to tell everyone you're back from college for the holidays; it will be the best surprise. I love you too, darling. See you shortly," a voice says from a room above me.

I feel like this voice is meant for me as well. It is my divine sign. With the gift from the angel tucked between my fingers, I begin to crawl, inch by inch, toward the entrance to the space between the walls. My decaying flesh catches on a nail, but I won't let it deter me. Not today.

I yearn to move up toward the warmth, the love, and the light. The light of hope. The light of holy fluorescence. The light of family. The light I can finally see. "Thank you," I cry.

Inch by painful inch, I stop to rest, to breathe. Something screeches and runs by my hand, but I am not afraid. Since the old man stopped coming, the rats have been my only companions these long years and my only meals, sent to me by the angels themselves to keep me going. I can see them now, though, their sleek, dark, furry bodies and surprisingly long fleshy tails. I know that the best bit of meat is at the haunches, though you must be careful not to puncture the innards. And be wary of the fleas. The fleas make you feel sick for a long, long time. Sores, fevers, swollen neck and armpits, and a long, long sleep. A sleep of the dead. I slept this sleep for years, a place between life and death, a place of rotting. It's hard to mind the fleas in the dark. They're already so small.

I move my desiccated body, dragging it over the hard-packed dirt that smells of mildew and eternal dampness and condensation, my skin stretched like an old canvas. I feel it rip upon the ground, paint chips, wood spears, and rusty nails, trying to keep me from leaving the home they made for me. My congealed blood oozes upon the broken bricks where I enter the space between the walls, my eyes fixated on the glow above. Up I climb. Up, up, up, toward the laughter and good cheer, the chatting of friends. Up toward the feasting of the family, and the food I can smell as I get closer.

I wonder if the old man is there, if perhaps he's not dead, and he will be surprised to see me. Surprised to see I was made whole once more by my beloved seraphim. It's been so long since the old man's been down to visit me. I wonder if you can ever truly forget the one whom you ripped away from their life and family. Why would God allow someone to take them, take their eyes, stash them away like an old box of papers in the basement, and forget they exist? The angel whispered in my ear, "To make you a martyr, Lucy."

I slither like an injured snake, all jutting curves and clumsy S shapes. I wonder if they can hear me now, clunking through the walls toward the warmth of their fire, the brilliance of their red and green twinkling lights. I am so close to them now, but so tired. I need to rest for a while. I close my renewed eyes and sleep for just a moment before I am awakened by a knock at the door, then voices.

"Hi, Mom! Sorry, I'm late. The light rail got delayed and had to switch tracks," the voice says.

"Oh, that's alright, sweetheart. I'm so glad you could make it this year! Ever since Grandpa died, the holidays just haven't felt the same. The saffron cakes are cooling on the stove. Come have one!"

I hear their footsteps and feel them move deeper within the house. I wriggle further in, my strength renewed, making my way toward the heart of the house. I know where I am now, and I know where I want to be.

The grate below the unused fireplace, sitting empty for the huge amount of creosote that has built up, growing for decades. "A fire hazard, a danger," the old man used to say.

I can hear the people now, the feasters gathered for St. Lucy's day. For *my* day. I will bring them the light. I will bring hope once more into these dark winter months. I will deliver sight to them like the angel did to me.

I slide my skeletal fingers between the gaps in the grate and push. At first, I don't think I have the strength to move it. Perhaps I have decayed too long below the floors, wasting away and forgotten. With the archangel's help, I push the metal grate to the side and slink upwards into the hearth. Even with my eyes, I still can't see it, but I can feel it there, assisting me.

As I rise into the fireplace, I admire the glow of the decorations and the food before me. It's all so beautiful. It's been so long since I've seen anything, and those were always my favorite parts of the Christmas season.

I rest my bones into a crouch, my skin mixing with the soot and tar of yesteryears, turning me black before it falls off with a damp plop. I didn't know my body could make such sounds anymore. Before me, on the stone ledge, sits the Santa Lucia crown, its white candles dusty and unused. Perhaps no one has worn this since my last feast day years ago. That makes me both happy and sad. Santa Lucy deserved better. I deserved better, too. I heave my decaying body from the hearth and unfurl myself like a dried flower.

"The light shines in the darkness, and the darkness has not overcome it," I say, my throat aflame with God's holy love, and desiccated from my time below.

Someone gasps, and the room grows silent but for a jaunty rendition of "God Rest Ye Merry Gentlemen" murmuring from the record player. A youth, a girl as I once was, spots me and points, her face aghast. I see faces lean in, necks craning to see me. And who can blame them? Who would deny themselves a glimpse of a miracle of God? I am Lady Lazarus; I spread my arms wide, presenting them with such sacred sights. Chairs scrape and clatter, silverware drops, and I see people moving frantically. Some run toward me, and others away, sprinting for the door.

"Oh, dear lord, is that … Is that … *Aunt Lucy*?"

Glorified to hear my name from someone's lips after so long, I part what is left of my own lips into a smile that twinkles with green rot in the glow from the Christmas tree. I pick up the crown and place it upon my head, the fleshless tips of my sharp fingers clicking against the antique metal which settles upon my patchy tresses with a sound like the chaffing of wheat. I take a match from the box the angel slipped into my hand, and one by one, I begin to light the candles. What's left of my hair goes up like a torch, setting me and the crown ablaze. I shamble from the fireplace toward my family, my arms outstretched, reaching for them, beckoning for a loving embrace. The wax drips down my face and onto the floor as I scamper, setting the old wooden floorboards ablaze.

With my arms outstretched, I beckon them to me. "Can you see the light? The glow? Feel the warmth? Isn't it beautiful?"

The candle wax splashes upon my newfound eyes, making it hard to see. It makes me anxious, the thought of losing sight again, but I trust the angel. I have brought its light to my family. Santa Lucy would be proud. I catch someone by the jacket and press them to my body in a fiery, blazing hug. My love for them is infinite, just like the Lord's love. I feel them catch fire as I squeeze, filling them with the love of God's glory. With this, their holy penance for their ignorance to my cries, for their blind eye to the old man's sins, I forgive them. God forgives them.

Their jacket falls to pieces upon the floor, their skin charring and blistering beneath the bones of my fingers. Everyone begins to scream. The waxen flames have reached my eyes, and they burn the sight from them. The angel has claimed back its gift now that I have achieved my purpose. I am a beacon of light and warmth. The house aflame around me, I crawl back to the hearth, back to my home beneath the basement, back to await the gift of sight and know God's light once more. The angel knows I'm worthy now, and I know it will come again.

H.V. PATTERSON

H.V. Patterson (she/her) lives in Oklahoma and writes speculative fiction, poetry, and plays. Recent publications include *Haven Speculative, Small Wonders, Flash Fiction Online,* and *Best Horror of the Year.* She's a cofounder of *Horns and Rattles Press*,

You can find her on
Bluesky @hvpatterson
Instagram@hvpattersonwriter
hvpatterson.com

WREN'S DAY
BY H.V. PATTERSON

Frances stared out the window as they drove by withered farmland, forlorn beneath a morose, gray sky. It was December 26th, the day after Frances's first, disastrous Christmas with Stephen's family, and the dreary Oklahoma landscape echoed the emptiness of her heart.

They were lost. They'd been lost since Stephen left the highway hours ago, insisting he knew a shortcut.

114

They passed a skeletal tree inhabited by a family of crows. Frances considered rolling down her window to hear their raucous caws, but Stephen drove over a jarring pothole and swore viciously. Frances froze, watching the birds vanish from sight. Stephen was in a terrible mood. If she moved, if she did anything at all, he would turn on her.

Frances had tried so hard, longing for love, yearning to be embraced by Stephen's enormous family. And for three, grueling days, her in-laws had made her their scapegoat. Stephen hadn't defended her once; he'd smirked at their viciousness. Frances had pretended everything was fine. She'd smiled in the family pictures, concealing how miserable she'd been, how many tears she'd repressed.

"Shit." Stephen smacked the steering wheel, and Frances flinched as the horn screamed. "We got ourselves lost," he declared.

He'd gotten them lost, but Frances kept her mouth shut. She'd discovered that Stephen was as magnanimous in sharing blame as he was selfish in hoarding credit.

It could be worse, Frances reminded herself, as she had over and over during Christmas. Stephen had a good job in IT. He could be sarcastic and cutting, but he never hit her or made her feel physically unsafe. He merely made it clear, with every resentful fiber of his being, that her presence was a burden, barely tolerated. That she was the albatross about his throat keeping him from whatever life he believed he deserved.

Frances had smoothed over the red-flags waving during their engagement, their wedding, and the first nine months of their marriage. But all the home-cooked meals she'd prepared after long days at the clinic, all the weekends she'd toiled, keeping the house spotless, had been taken for granted and never appreciated. She'd been building her nest in quicksand.

What had she expected, anyway? What did she know about building a healthy relationship? Her only models were couples in Hallmark movies. Her mother and aunts were divorced and dead. Her grandmother was a divorced, destitute, resentful invalid who refused to speak to Frances, her only remaining family.

"Well?" Stephen asked impatiently, like she owed him an explanation.

"Look, a gas station," Frances said, grateful for the distraction. "We need to fill up, right? We can ask for directions while we're there."

Stephen frowned and grunted. But he pulled over without any cutting remarks.

"You should run along to the restroom," he said. "You girls and your bladders." He chuckled as he exited the car.

Frances stared at Stephen's retreating back. His blond hair was carefully combed over a small bald patch at the crown of his head. Stephen would be as bald as his father before he turned 40. He'd find some way to blame her for that, too.

She didn't have to use the restroom, but she knew Stephen would weaponize her lack of obedience if she didn't comply. As she unfolded herself from the cramped car and stepped into the cold air, a wedge of geese in V-formation soared far above, softly honking. Frances wondered if they ever felt lonely. Was it possible to be lonely in such a large, noisy flock? Of course it was; she'd spent the last three days with a great, noisy family, feeling lonelier than ever.

Her hands itched for her binoculars, but she'd buried them in her closet. Stephen had mocked her bird watching so often that she'd stopped, though the hobby had given her much solace, and bird song had once quickened something in her heart. She'd once proudly called herself a bird person. Now, she didn't call herself anything but a wife and clinic manager.

The geese vanished from sight. If Frances had wings, she, too, would migrate to better wintering grounds. The sun had crept low in the sky. It would be dark soon. Stephen loitered at the counter in the gas station, probably waiting for the clerk. Frances couldn't bring herself to go into the restroom or climb back into the car. Even though she knew Stephen would have something sarcastic to say about her wandering, she drifted up a nearby rise and found herself looking down on a town.

The town was close, less than half a mile away. It gleamed in the early evening light, all red brick and fresh paint. Booths covered in food and drinks surrounded a large central square. In the center of the square, a massive pile of timber waited to blaze in a merry bonfire. People milled about, hanging bright, green wreaths and gaudy ribbons, preparing to celebrate something. Maybe an after Christmas festival? A slight breeze carried their voices to her, their chatter interspersed with laughter.

Frances wished, again, for her binoculars. It would be spying, but she'd love to see the glowing faces which must accompany those cheerful voices and bustling, purposeful movements. The whole scene reminded her of the Hallmark movies in which small towns were always welcoming places full of wholesome, community-minded folks—no poverty, no simmering resentment, no passive-aggressive sniping. Those movies used to give her hope that the life she yearned for was out there, somewhere, waiting for her.

Frances knew she'd been naïve to yearn for a Hallmark movie Christmas with Stephen's family, to hope that marriage could mean stepping into a story where kindness, hard work, and good intentions won you appreciation and love.

And yet, she gazed at the prosperous town with yearning.

Maybe she could coax Stephen into stopping there for dinner. Maybe she could soak up some of the cheer radiating from below for an hour or so.

Children shouted and shrieked behind her. Frances reluctantly wrenched herself from idle daydreams and turned towards the noise.

A procession of children milled across the road. Hundreds of children dressed in bright, gaudy clothes laughing, shouting, singing, chanting, screaming like a colony of belligerent gulls. There were no adults, and none of the children looked older than twelve. Some waddled along with the uneven gait of toddlers barely winning the fight against gravity. Where had they all come from? She and Stephen hadn't passed them on the road. Such a massive group of noisy, exuberant children would've been impossible to miss.

Despite their energetic noise, the group moved at a deliberate pace. As they approached, Frances realized they were following a small bird that hopped slowly down the dirt road, one wing dragging uselessly on the ground.

Frances waited for the children to help the bird. It was clearly injured and scrambling away from the noisy throng. And the children knew it was there; they were keeping pace behind it like hounds on a trail.

The bird faltered maybe 20 feet from Frances, sides heaving with exhaustion. A tall, dark-haired girl knelt, grabbed a handful of gravel from the side of the road, and tossed it at the bird. It cheeped wretchedly then continued hopping forward. Several children hooted and jeered at the suffering bird.

Frances waited for someone to intervene, to order the children to stop. But there were no other adults, just her. She hurried forward—but something jerked her back. It was Stephen, his large, rough hand wrapped around her arm.

"Leave it alone, Frances," he ordered. "The damned station isn't staffed so I can't get directions. But I filled up at the pump. Let's get out of here."

"They're hurting it!" Frances said, tugging against his relentless grip.

A few children glanced at them and waved. Stephen waved back, smiling as he hissed, "For God's sakes, Frances, it's just a bird. It's not our business."

Stephen started towing her back to the car, expecting compliance. But fury unfurled within Frances. How dare he treat her like a recalcitrant child, like she was in the wrong when a bird was being tortured? She yanked herself free, stormed through the throng of children, and picked up the bird.

The bird shivered against Frances while she checked it for injuries. One wing was definitely broken. She stroked the crown of its tiny head. As it scrutinized her with bright, liquid eyes, the part of her brain that had never stopped loving birds, despite Stephen's disparaging remarks, awoke. She held the small, round bird with reddish-brown plumage on top and a paler belly. White lines of feathers arched from its eyes like dramatic eyeliner. Its slender beak was slightly downturned, giving it a somber, aggrieved air. He was—the females had duller plumage—a Carolina Wren.

"Ma'am, please put the wren down," said the tall girl who'd thrown the gravel. Her voice was polite, as if she were asking Frances to pass the potatoes.

"How can you torture an animal?" Frances demanded, cradling the bird protectively against her sweater. "Where are your parents? They would be ashamed of you!"

"You're from out of town," the girl said, as if this explained everything. "I understand how this looks. But ma'am, this is The Harrowing of the Wren. Our parents know where we are and what we're doing. They're waiting for us." The girl pointed down the road to the bustling town.

"See, Frances? Their parents know," Stephen called, arms crossed. He kept his tone light, but once they were alone, he would tell Frances exactly how much she had embarrassed him.

"Ma'am, please," the girl stepped forward, hand outstretched like Frances was a skittish, feral creature in need of soothing.

Frances stepped back, cradling the wren against her throat. His soft feathers tickled her chin. His panicked heart thrummed against her skin.

"Frances!" Stephen snapped, dropping all pretense. He stalked onto the road, stirring up clouds of dust with every angry step. "Put that filthy thing down and get in the car."

Adrenaline surged through Frances. Should she run? She wasn't in terrible shape, but she couldn't outrun all these children. She could call the police, but they'd never get here in time, if they even took her seriously. They'd probably parrot what Stephen had said: it's just a bird; its life doesn't matter.

As Stephen reached for her, Frances stepped off the road to the withered field on the other side. There was no wind, no sound of other animals. Even the children were unnaturally still. She snarled at Stephen, the harsh sound cutting through the sudden silence.

Stephen retreated to the center of the road, staring at Frances like she was a stranger. Maybe she was. He'd never been interested in her authentic self. He'd always seen her as a defective extension of his own will.

"There must be a wren," the girl said into the ringing silence.

She reached into her pocket and pulled out a stone. The other children mimicked her, pulling stones from pockets, bags, and hidden places. The girl gazed assessingly at Frances as she turned the stone over in her palm.

Stephen didn't understand his peril until the girl lobbed the stone at his head with the practiced ease of a seasoned pitcher. It cracked against his forehead, and he gasped, hands fumbling at the bloody gash. Before he could retreat, another stone slammed into the bridge of his nose. He grunted and staggered back. He turned to flee, but it was too late. Frances watched, paralyzed, as stones volleyed into Stephen. He crashed to his knees, screaming, futilely trying to shield himself from the merciless barrage. Dozens, then hundreds of stones piled up around him. The assault didn't falter until Stephen fell, moaning, onto the road.

The children stopped and stared at Stephen's wheezing body, waiting for something.

Frances willed her legs to move, but she was exhausted and trembling with unused adrenaline. And the wren was so heavy in her arms. She should—what? Defend Stephen from this mob? Impossible. She should run from these children, from Stephen, from the town. She should call 911 as she fled back to a world that made sense.

But a vicious part of Frances didn't want to help Stephen. Hadn't he dragged them out to Oklahoma for his family's Christmas? And hadn't he insisted this was a shortcut despite her reservations? She'd wanted to spend a quiet holiday at home—but Stephen always got his way, and he always ran roughshod over her suggestions, treating them like personal attacks on his intelligence.

Stephen convulsed, blood-streaked limbs tossing up a cloud of dust. Haloed by the cloud, Stephen folded in on himself. He loosed a burbling cry, like a bird being strangled. His eyes withered like raisins in his collapsing face. His mouth distended, sharpened, jutted into a beak. His hair darkened into reddish-brown feathers. He grew smaller and smaller—then vanished. His hollowed-out clothes held the memory of his ghost for a moment before collapsing.

Something struggled at the collar of Stephen's coat. A bird, another Carolina Wren, thrashed its way free from the clothes. It hobbled onto the dirt and cheeped mournfully, one wing dragging.

The wren in Frances's arms grew bigger, his warm, soft body overfilling her hands.

"Ma'am?" the girl said solicitously, as if the impossible hadn't happened. "We must have a wren for the harrowing."

The wren that had been Stephen lurched towards Frances. But the children hemmed it in and drove it back to the center of the road.

"I know this is a shock," the girl continued. "But you have to choose."

The wren in Frances's hands grew larger and heavier. Her shoulders creaked in protest. The wren weighed more than a baby, a toddler. He was too heavy to hold. She knelt, and the wren-thing sprawled half on her lap, half onto brittle grass. Feathers shrank and vanished. His beak melted back into his head and reformed into a mouth. Dark hair replaced feathers.

A naked man sprawled on the ground, head in Frances's lap, broken arm cradled protectively against his chest. The man's gray-green eyes gazed at Frances like she was a saint, descended from heaven to grant him absolution.

"Have you chosen?" the girl asked.

Frances wrenched her gaze from the man to the road. The girl stood, waiting for an answer, while the other children flowed around her, driving the wren towards town. The wren burbled protests and tried to escape, but it was harried on all sides.

"Why?" Frances asked.

"It's Wren's Day, Ma'am," the girl said.

Frances had never heard of Wren's Day. But the words clanged through her mind like ringing bells. She considered the prosperous-looking town preparing for a festival, the procession of laughing children, the man-turned-wren.

All these pieces were connected to this Wren's Day. A holiday, a holy day. And what were most holy days? Days to commemorate or renew a sacrifice. After all, sacrifice lay at the heart of almost everything.

Frances recognized the nuances and demands of sacrifice. Day after day for nine long months, she'd made sacrifices of her time, her wellbeing, very self, to keep the peace with Stephen, to present the façade of a loving, happy marriage.

"I've chosen," Frances said, wrapping one hand protectively around the naked stranger's shoulders.

The girl nodded. "We'll see you both in town," she said. "Everyone will be happy to meet you."

The girl moved away, resuming her place at the head of the procession. She started singing in a language Frances didn't know. Some children joined in. Others laughed, chanted, jeered, screamed.

"Hello," the man croaked. Despite the pain he must be in, his voice was as soft and gentle as his eyes.

"Hello," Frances said, suddenly shy. He was beautiful beneath the blood and grime.

What was wrong with her? Her husband's discarded clothes lay mere feet away. Her husband was being herded— harrowed—to his death. She should be crying, screaming, fighting. She shouldn't feel this strange surge of hope, this sense of a new beginning. She shouldn't be sacrificing her husband for this stranger whose name she didn't even know.

"I'm Chris," the man said, easing onto his knees.

"Frances." She already missed the weight of his head in her lap. The man shivered. "You must be cold," she said.

Frances stood and walked to her former husband's clothes. They were torn and trampled, covered with blood, broken feathers, and stones. She shook the coat out, helped Chris to his feet, and draped the coat over him. It would offer some protection. He clutched it closed as best he could with his good arm.

Frances grabbed the jeans, tattered as they were, and helped Chris step into them, blushing and averting her eyes. Next came the shoes, barely scuffed from their ordeal. Chris hopped awkwardly as she slid the shoes over his battered feet. Everything fit him perfectly.

"I'm much obliged to you, Frances," he said.

"It's nothing." She stood, wiping dirt onto her grubby sweater.

"I don't just mean about the clothes," Chris said.

"I know," Frances said. "Really, it's nothing. He was … he wasn't always a good man."

Chris nodded solemnly.

"He'll make a good wren," he said. "There must be a wren."

"To keep the town flourishing," Frances said, nodding. "There's always sacrifice at the heart of every beautiful thing."

"Yes, that's it, exactly!" He smiled warmly, all surprised delight. "You understand."

"I didn't, for years," Frances confessed.

"We all grow up at some point," Chris said gently.

Frances placed her hand on his shoulder. Even through the coat, she could feel his warmth. She remembered how he'd felt as a bird, nestled against her throat, and an irrational surge of affection flooded her. She'd just met Chris. And her husband … she shouldn't feel this way while her former husband was marching to his grave.

And yet, Frances felt like she'd known Chris her whole life. Was he faking the warmth radiating from his eyes and soft smile? She didn't think so.

All the faults of her past marriage were so clear now. What she'd thought of as mutual respect and love had been nothing but condescension on her former husband's part and a desperate, cringing submission on hers.

This was different. It had to be. This was true love at first sight.

"Do you have any family?" Chris asked.

She shook her head.

"My family will be real happy to meet you," he said. "I hope you'll—that is, you're welcome to stay."

Frances didn't know what awaited her in this town, or even its name. But hadn't the town already laid its darkness before her and shown her plainly what sacrifices it would demand? She gazed into Chris's eyes and imagined summers of lush grass, winters spent cuddling together, skin pressed to

EMILY J. WEISENBERGER

Emily J. Weisenberger (she/her) is a fiction writer for children and adults. Her short stories are published in Tales to Terrify, L'Esprit Literary Review, and The Vanishing Point, among others. She is an MFA candidate in creative writing and the fiction editor of the intersectional feminist magazine So To Speak. Her prior education is in anthropology.

Author Website: emilyjweisenberger.com
My Bluesky: @ejweisenberger.bsky.social

THE WATCHER AT HER BACK

BY EMILY J. WEISENBERGER

Shira reads the invitation to the charity bike ride and texts back: NO!

Then she adds a frowny face to soften the blow because no matter how hard she tries to cut herself off from Avi, she's afraid she still needs him. Her therapists, all of them, have told her it's only a phobia. Just this morning, one said, "Safety is a state of mind. You create it, not him."

Avi replies less than a minute later: Come on! It's been months. You have to miss biking by now.

Then he says: You know I always watch your back Sheer.

Shira grinds her teeth as his words take effect on her. Even his presence in a text can light up those deep, calming networks in her mind.

"I don't need him," she chants to herself. "I'm an adult."

It's bizarre to think that Avi was ever a stranger to her. Shira met him on the beach in Yorktown, Virginia. It was race day, nine years ago. She was a teenager.

There was a pre-dawn start to beat the heat, and the weak light climbing over the horizon barely bisected the massing gray water from the sky, but still a photographer forced the cyclists to dip the back wheels of their bikes into the York River for a posed shot.

The sandy river floor sucked at Shira's bare feet, and she struggled to keep hold of her bike—No, Lessie's bike. It was Lessie's bike she was using.

Shira death-gripped the handlebars against the swill of the water and tried not to imagine her parents' reaction when they found out she was competing in the Transamerica Bike

Race. Mom and Dad were still asleep in Lessie's hospital room when Shira had snuck out. When they woke up to see her on the news, they would think she was crazy, possessed by a dybbuk, spirit-led.

But Shira knew it was belief in the power of biking, not Lessie's wandering spirit, that led her away from her sister's comatose body and onto her bike. Maybe, Shira had thought, if she did this absurd race, Lessie would wake up. But the idea of getting back out on the road, now that she'd seen how dangerous it really was . . .

Avi, a nameless man then, stood with his bike to Shira's left. He pointed at her helmet, under which her braids were already wet with nervous sweat, and said, "That's too loose for you."

Shira choked, trying to stanch sudden tears, but she couldn't help it. The car crash had been only two days prior.

Shira had been biking ahead of Lessie on a short ride down the Colonial Parkway. Lessie had said it would be an easy one, a way to stay fresh before the race. A few miles in, a pickup truck steamed around the bend behind them. Shira noticed it in the mirror that hung from her helmet. Her big sister looked so small in comparison to the truck, pedaling on the road's shoulder, but even then, Shira could see the strength and grace that drove her sister's whole being.

The engine roared the driver's impatience. There was a shout from Lessie—"Sheer!" it could have been, but she couldn't really hear—and then her sister's body disappeared from the mirror, and all that was left was the truck, swerving away, the driver red-faced and cursing.

Without asking, Avi reached over to tighten Shira's helmet strap just as the camera flashed.

Avi biked that race with Shira, trailing her from the start line. She not once asked him to, but after he caught her crying at the start line, after she admitted she was terrified she'd get hit by a car just like her big sister, he said, "I'll watch your back." He watched her back the whole 3,000-plus miles from the East Coast to the West.

How grateful she was to Avi during that first race, when there was still hope Lessie would wake up, and all Shira had to do was pedal westward to the finish line. If she could just finish it, she told herself. If she could finish it—a miracle—then Lessie might wake up. A miracle for a miracle.

She has never been able to bike out on a road without him since. Not with her "phobia." There are sponsors who want to bring her to training camps in Mallorca and Adelaide. Coaches who want to work with her, make her the best solo cyclist in the world. But how can she do that without the help of a man she doesn't want in her life?

***

Shira still hasn't replied to his text by the next morning, but that hasn't stopped Avi from sending her another: **Did you see it's a charity ride to raise money for BIKE LANES? That is so your thing.**

Shira sets down her spoon—she was eating breakfast—and flops her head into her hands. He's right. He's right. He's always right.

I'm the same age now that you were on the day we met, Shira texts back.

His reply is quick. **Reminiscing? That's only going to make you sad </3**

I was already sad.

So does this mean you're coming? Avi asks. **I make you feel better.**

Shira leaves him on read.

Shira's home gym—her garage—has no windows and only one naked bulb, so the exercise machines, free weights, and spare bike parts cast stark shadows over all four walls. On the wall, hanging from hooks like a prized heirloom, is

Lessie's old bike. It's dusty from months of disuse, and there's a cobweb on the handlebar.

On a peg beside the bike is the cracked helmet Lessie was wearing during the crash. It hangs in a shadow, as if covered in a gray shroud. Shira acknowledges Lessie's cracked helmet like she would a mezuzah: she kisses her fingers, places them on the helmet, then brings her fingers back to her lips. It's how she says hi to her sister.

Shira takes down Lessie's bike. She wipes the seat and scratched frame and tests the brakes and gear shifts. After a few adjustments, she's sure they're all working fine. She adds air to the tires, pulls on her own helmet, and adjusts the clip-on mirror.

The garage door clangs upward on its track. Winter's chill air rolls into the garage and hits Shira in the face. She readies herself, swings a leg over Lessie's bike. She hasn't ridden it since this summer, when she and Avi finished the Paris-Brest-Paris. It was their third record-breaking ride as an ultra-long distance cycling duo.

"I don't need him. I create my safety." Her tongue tastes the sweat on her lips.

She stands over her bike and watches a car careen by on the road out front. There's silence in the neighborhood for a while, then two more cars go through. In the next car that drives by, someone waves from the driver's seat. Her muscles cool and stiffen. She shivers.

She counts 13 more cars until she gives up and closes the garage door.

Shira covers both eyes with her fists and groans into the empty garage. She puts Lessie's bike back up on its rack and returns, like she does every day, to training on the stationary bike.

She pedals intently, hitting her target pace with relish. After a dozen or so miles, her muscles turn hot with pain, so hot it feels like they could tear. It is always in this pain, when she's ragged and overheated from exertion, pedaling on the last threads of her energy, that Shira feels closest to her big sister.

She keeps pedaling, feels the sheering of her muscles ramp up, and the chafing between her thighs, the blisters forming where she grips the handlebars. The harder she goes, the more the hurt feels right.

Hours go by. The odometer surpasses the 80-mile mark. Shira should stop to eat. She's only had breakfast today. Her panting is breathy and gasping, like when she's been crying desperately, and her skin feels tingly and loose. Darkness caresses the edges of her vision, seems to spill down from the ceiling.

Shira remembers finding herself on the Colonial Parkway standing over Lessie's bike, which lay chain-side down in the grass on the side of the road. The back wheel spun, tick-tick-ticking. Shira had the thought that Lessie would be pissed if it turned out the bike was damaged. Lessie had been prepping for the Transamerica Bike Race since winter break. Had actually dropped out of college, which Lessie'd announced to their tearful parents on New Year's Eve, to save up money for the fancy road bike.

The bike seemed in okay shape. Dinged up, but she figured Lessie could still ride it on race day.

Then she had found Lessie. She was lying face-up in the ditch. Her helmet was cracked and—"Lessie! Lessie wake up!"—and there was something funny with her head. Shira yanked the helmet off. Her sister's head was the wrong shape. Dented, like a bumper.

Shira grips the handlebars of the stationary bike and shrieks into the empty garage. She shrieks until her breath runs out, and then she breathes in and shrieks again.

"Why couldn't it be you who watches my back? LESSIE!"

The cracked helmet up on the peg moves. Nothing as ostentatious as rattling. It shivers, and like smoke from a smokestack, a shadow fills the air above it.

"Sheer," the shadow moans.

Shira gasps, scrambles off the stationary bike, its wheels spiraling without her, and trips backwards onto the concrete floor. She watches with horror as the massing shadow moves toward her, spilling over itself to reach her.

Then it stops short. It is tethered to the helmet.

The mass shudders and groans as it tries to yank itself closer to Shira, but then it seems to grow tired, and it stops.

"Sheer?" it says more quietly.

Only two people call Shira that, and only one of them is alive. So this shadow must be—It must be, "Lessie?"

"Sheer," the dybbuk of Shira's older sister says.

"Lessie, oh my god."

Shira scrabbles closer to the dark dybbuk. She reaches out with her fingers. As she touches it, she feels loved as only a younger sister can be loved by the older. It is better than Avi watching her back. It is the safest feeling in the world.

"You came to me," Shira says. "You came back. Lessie. Lessie! I finished that race for you. Nine years. I biked across the whole country. It was crazy. I wish"—Shira truly begins to sob—"you were the one I biked with. I've never stopped wishing you were there."

Lessie's spirit writhes in apparent distress.

"Sheer," Lessie says, and then with what seems to be an enormous effort, "Listen."

***

On December 30th, a southbound train carries Shira from Maryland to Avi's town in Florida. She will be there early for the charity bike ride on New Year's Eve. Beside her, Lessie's old bike rocks to the sway of the train and tracks black grease marks onto her jeans, but Shira doesn't mind. It feels right having it close.

Soon after dusk, the train pulls in to a station lit with glowing holiday lights. Tinsel snakes around lampposts. It's that sleepy time of year when everyone is coming down from the high of the holidays, so the small crowd of travelers is slow moving.

Shira rolls her bike into the pick-up area. Her bike ticks beside her. The Florida heat rises from the blacktop in humid waves. She finds Avi, with his bike, leaning against a no-parking sign.

"Hey," he says. He's still the same as he ever was. Still lanky and straight-faced. Bike grease stains his fingertips, and the cycling cap pushes down his scraggly hair. All these years, and he hasn't changed.

Shira is the one who initiates a hug, one arm wrapping around his back, the other balancing her bike. She knew he would meet her at the station, even though she hadn't asked.

He kisses her temple. A familiar calm settles into her. A sense only Avi, since Lessie's death, has been able to give her. It's like sitting under a sturdy tree in a windstorm. Outside of its canopy, the world is terrifying, but beneath it, she is protected. She closes her eyes.

They pull back, and he says, "Do you remember the way?"

"To your parents' house? Of course."

If Avi is their team's protector, she is their compass and their engine. Shira has always been the one to map the rides, set the tempos, and shelter Avi from the headwind. They both know he's a good cyclist, but that Shira is a great one. If he didn't draft off her wake, he would gas out before the finish line.

Shira walks her bike onto the road. Avi is there behind her, like always, like she needs. The white light strapped to his handlebar pulses in her helmet mirror, a sign of his canopy enveloping her.

She relaxes onto the saddle and pushes off, gliding into the weightless, relentlessly forward motion of biking. They pedal through the town center where logs are stacked up for the New Year's bonfire. They pass the shopping center where drivers honk and shoot out into the road and forget their turn signals. But Avi is there to protect her. Never once during the ride does Shira worry about getting hit.

When they arrive, Avi's parents are ebullient and warm as always.

"Jackie! Our daughter is here!" Devin calls over his shoulder as he opens the door. "How long are you staying, honey? I want to hear how you've been." He holds a hand out for Shira's backpack.

She gives it to him with a, "Thanks, Devin. Do you mind if I bring my bike in?"

"Of course not," he says. He nudges the cat with his foot and it scampers up the stairs. "Hey, when do I get to cheer you on next? Avi tells me the dream team doesn't have a race lined up yet."

Shira says, "Yeah, no I'm thinking about trying something new this year. Maybe going solo."

Devin's eyes flick up to his son, who is holding the screen door open behind Shira.

Avi says, "We'll see. We still have to decide what to do next."

"Well whatever you decide, you know we'll come cheer you on. Whether Avi's with you or not," Devin says and cups Shira's shoulder.

Shira's own parents don't cheer her on. They have always gritted their teeth whenever Shira's pro-cycling career comes up. They use words like 'extreme' and 'nuts' to describe it. But Avi's parents kvell about Shira's and Avi's successes. It makes Shira both grateful and nervous. How sure Devin and Jackie are that Shira and Avi will both go on biking and living. How little they think about looking over shoulders for death steaming around the corner.

In Jackie and Devin's front hall, a photo hangs behind glass. Shira hated to look at it, always let her eyes slide over the glass on the way into the kitchen. But today, she stops to examine it, and Avi stops and looks with her too. She feels him behind her body.

It's the first ever photo of the two of them together, the one taken at the York River. In the image, a line of proud cyclists smiles to the camera, except for Shira and Avi on the end. Avi has hold of Shira's helmet in his slender left hand. His right tests the tension of the chin strap. Shira is tilting toward his hand, so her face is covered, her tears unrecorded. His beard is scraggly and his face is dark with sunburn. He exudes a strength wound tightly in his lanky frame.

It was cut out of the newspaper, probably by Devin, so the caption is visible across the bottom of the photo. Rising star Shira Halpern, 17, competes solo in the Transamerica Bike Race 2 days after the car crash that put her sister, teammate Alessandra Halpern into a coma.

Shira remembers how it felt when Avi's fingers hooked under the strap of her helmet, how he held her together. It would be so easy to lean into him, to give up her solo dreams and just agree to do what Avi wants. His body heat radiates behind her. She steps around him and walks into the kitchen.

Shira is ushered to the table where two Shabbat candles are already burning. Four glasses of red wine mark each place setting.

"Darling!" Jackie cries to Shira.

"Hey Jackie. Thanks for having me."

"Of course. You're always welcome here." Jackie's hug envelopes Shira in the yeasty scent of freshly baked challah.

Dinner is pleasant, with the brisket and stewed carrots melting deliciously on Shira's tongue. Jackie reminds them all to stock up on carbs. "Twenty-six miles! We need our energy." That's how long the charity bike ride is: 26 miles for the year 2026. Jackie tears off more challah and passes the loaf to Devin.

Avi catches Shira's eye, and she has to try not to laugh. That distance is nothing for pro-cyclists like them.

Avi's parents fill Shira in on their health, on the cat's antics with the poor birds in the front yard, on how Avi has been lazing around without Shira to push him to train. The meal lasts so long, they all head straight upstairs after washing up. Avi goes to take a shower. Jackie and Devin disappear into their bedroom.

Alone, Shira carries her backpack and bike up the stairs and into her room. She roots through her backpack for pajamas and a toothbrush. The bag is pretty bulky with one helmet—hers—clipped to the outside, and a second inside the main pouch. She pulls the second helmet out.

"Lessie," Shira whispers to it. "Are you there? I don't know if—"

A sliver of shadow trickles from the crack in the helmet like a blown-out candle.

Shira stares. What happened in the garage was really real. It was. The dybbuk she saw, it really—*Lessie* really—

The shower squeaks off. Out in the hall, the bathroom door whooshes open. Shira feels a draft over her bare feet as the air is sucked out from under the door.

Shira jerks back. She's panting a bit, and sweat is prickling her armpits. She hides the helmet back in her bag and gets up to lock the door; Avi has a habit of coming in without knocking.

Sometime in the night, Shira wakes to the sound of Avi turning the handle. The door rocks against the frame and the lock holds. He taps on the door. "Sheer," he hisses, "let me in."

Out of habit, Shira almost gets up to let him, but she manages to lie still, hoping he leaves. She remembers the first time he came into her room. After they met in Yorktown, Shira had returned home to Maryland, watched Lessie fade and die, watched her parents fade and grieve, and taken up running. Running was safer. Running was done on sidewalks or tracks, and it was almost as good as biking.

But she could never get far enough on just her own two feet. A bike took you new places. A bike gave you the world. Running just meant striking the same stretch of the Earth until you ran your knees down to the nubs. By the summer after her senior year of high school, Shira had had enough. She sent an email to Avi with the subject line: Can I come? I want to bike. He said yes, and she took a train down to stay with an older man she barely knew and his parents.

It was like coming home. Shira and Avi biked up and down the coastline, through misty forested paths hung with vines, across wooden boardwalks that rumbled beneath them, to a private cove among a stand of trees. They biked every day, all day, for weeks, and then Shira decided that she would cross Canada. She had crossed America by bike. She could do Canada, too. Avi had to come of course; she still couldn't shake off her phobia, but that didn't matter much to her then. She was just grateful she'd found a way to bike again.

It was the night after they'd made these plans that Avi had come into her room. She'd woken up to a body sliding beside hers. She was shocked. What was going on? He was her biking partner, her guardian on the road, but never her lover. She remembers how it felt to have his bony fame dig into her side, his beard tickle her neck, his fingers pull at her flesh. How it left her cold and confused at night and yet made her more worried, in the morning, that she needed him watching her back.

In time, though, Shira grew to accept this was a part of their relationship too, and eventually, after they finished the Trans Canada Trail, she thought they must be in love. That must be what her need for him meant.

But no. She's older now. Old enough to realize, finally, that there is something off in their partnership. Something tainted.

She turns onto her stomach. The coils of the twin-sized mattress creak as she spreads out to take all of its space for herself. Avi tries the handle a few more times.

She gets up, tip-toeing, but not to let him in. She has decided. She will ready herself for tomorrow. Shira goes to her bag and clips Lessie's cracked helmet onto the handlebars of her bike.

***

The charity ride's 26-mile route will start and end in the town center. Shira, Avi, Jackie, and Devin make it there early, so that Jackie and Devin can take Shira around to all their friends.

"We have a special guest with us!" Devin will pull someone aside with.

"Our Shira," Jackie will add. "She's a professional cyclist. This summer, she and Avi set a new record at a very important race in France."

"So nice to meet you!" their friend will exclaim.

Then Devin and Jackie will chatter about her a bit longer before finding another friend to socialize Shira with.

At one point in this process, Jackie leans into Shira and says, "You're quiet today. Everything alright?"

"Oh." Shira gives her a small smile. "No, nothing's wrong. Just didn't sleep much last night."

"You know," Jackie says, "Devin told me you might be going solo." She leans back to take in Shira. "I'm proud of you."

"Thanks Jackie. That means a lot." She pulls the older woman into a hug.

Jackie whispers, "Don't tell Avi I said this, but I think sometimes we just have to strike out on our own. Right?"

Tears prickle in Shira's eyes as she nods into the warmth of Jackie's embrace.

The ride is about to start. The square is ringed in string lights and palm trees. In the center is wood for the bonfire, to be ignited at dusk. A banner is hung between two of the trees imploring everyone to "Have a Very Happy New Year." Spectators lounge in folding chairs and pass around collecting boxes that jingle with coins.

People converge on the start line. Shira spots beach cruisers and tricycles and recumbent bikes. Bike enthusiasts of all kinds out to raise money for bike lanes.

There's a hush, then a horn goes, and the mass of bicyclists slowly picks up speed.

It feels as right as always to bike. To make the air pick up against her body. To work for it, to push and push and for her heartbeat to rise in response. She glances in her mirror, sees Avi pedaling behind her. His canopy a taut tether.

In the first few miles, Shira pedals through the throng ahead of Avi and his parents. As they turn onto Beach Drive and the buildings begin to drop away into aquamarine ocean and pale beaches, Shira breaks out in front.

She loves being in the front. In Florida, the roads are long and flat, and with no one ahead of her, the way is open and visible, beckoning her to come, come, come closer and see what there is to see. The ocean susurrates to her left. Miles pass almost as fast as minutes.

"I create my own safety. I create my own safety." These words taste like pennies, like hard work. Shira knows hard work.

At mile 18, Shira takes a right turn off the route into a stand of mangroves and cypress trees. She doesn't look back; Avi will follow her on a diversion, no matter where she leads him.

Shira bumps across the barely-there trail with Lessie's cracked helmet swinging wildly from the handlebars. Soon the sand gets too thick, and she has to walk the rest of the way. Only a couple minutes more and she emerges from the trees' shade into a small inlet, their secret cove.

Pale sand basks beneath clear, shallow water which ripples like a tiny, muted ocean. The flora—taller trees as well as grasses, saltbushes, palmettos, and sea grapes—make almost a full ring around the little cove, so the air is humid and briny, and it is private enough that boaters will have trouble seeing it, or anything happening in it.

Shira makes a seat in the sand. She pulls her bike along beside her and wraps her arm around the handlebars where the cracked helmet hangs, almost like she would wrap an arm around a friend's shoulders. Tiny fish, so small she could mistake them for glitter, flick through the water before her.

The sound of Avi pushing his bike over brush reaches her before he does.

"Do you remember the first time you took me here?" Shira says.

Avi grunts and sits down on her other side. "It's where we made plans to do the Trans Canada Trail. I was sitting there." He points to Shira. "And you were here."

Shira turns to look at the man she's known since childhood. "Thank you," she says, "for always watching my back. I do mean that."

"Well, a scared little girl like you, what else could I do? You needed me."

"Not anymore."

Avi sighs. "Come on, Sheer. Don't lie to yourself. I know you haven't biked without me. Not since—"

"Not since Lessie's accident. You're right. Nine years, and I'm still scared. But I'm not a little girl anymore."

Avi lets out a breath. "Doesn't mean you don't need protecting." He puts a hand on her leg where her biking shorts meet her thigh. "You said it yourself you like me watching your back."

She pushes his hand off.

He frowns. "After all I've done for you? What happened to you? This used to be so easy."

"I grew up, Avi. I'm 26. That's what happened." Shira stands up.

He shakes his head. "We're a team Sheer. More than a team." He looks up at her as she stands over him.

Avi doesn't know what Shira would do to go biking without him. Really biking. Pounding the road smooth beneath her wheels, curling the Earth's gusty breath around her body, chasing the horizon. Oh god, how she misses it. She is trapped, like a child who can never grow up. Either on a stationary bike or with Avi at her back, she is trapped. But there is another way. The dybbuk said so.

Only a few short minutes later, a man screams.

A shadowy cloud, like darkest smoke, rises above the cove. It shudders and writhes and begins to dissipate. Soon, it is so faint, it can no longer be seen. The sky is a brilliant, bright blue.

***

"LESSIE!" Shira had shrieked that cold winter's day in the garage, and something had answered.

"I need—I can only—" the dybbuk, Lessie, had said, "I must have a body."

Shira had the answer. It was brilliant, icy white, in Shira's mind. "If I get you a body, what happens to him? Will he become like you?"

"A dybbuk," Lessie confirmed.

But Shira couldn't summon pity for him. Avi had seen her crushed by fear and grief and full up of childish naiveté, and he had taken advantage. He had never asked. Not for the things he gave her or the things he took away.

"I can go see him on New Year's Eve," Shira said to her sister's spirit. "But how do I get you into his body?"

"That's the hard part."

"What do I have to do?" Shira asked.

"Kill him."

***

Even with the excursion to the secret cove, Shira wins the charity bike ride. She gets a shiny ribbon for her efforts and a photo with the mayor, who announces the ride raised more money than their stretch goal. The mayor is red-cheeked saying, "You all have done so much good today!"

At sundown, the bonfire goes up. Its crackling heat and cheery light suffuse the town center with a sort of golden aura. Kids bike in circles around each other, playing games of dare and balance. People make s'mores over fire pits. Adults pass around bottles of champagne, and as the night gets older, bottles of liquor.

Before midnight, Avi's parents decide to walk back home, and Shira and Avi follow, pushing their bikes. They turn into the neighborhood as the fireworks begin to go off.

"*Hap*-py New Year!" Devin shouts. He loops his arm through Jackie's.

Shira grabs Avi's arm in hers. "Happy New Year! Jackie, Devin, we have to tell you something."

She shares a smile with Avi. A purple bruise crosses below his chin like the outline of a helmet strap.

"Yes, darling?" Jackie says, sing-song.

A trio of fireworks boom-boom-crackle in the sky. A golden glow flashes over everyone's faces.

"Avi's going to help me train for my solo career!" Shira cries.

Jackie leans across Devin and says, "Attagirl."

Devin says, "Good on you, son. About time you helped her out rather than freeloading, huh?"

Avi nods at his father. He's quieter than usual, hasn't said a word in hours, and is a little clumsy in his lanky body. It could be because he's tired from the charity bike ride.

Back at the house, after the fireworks have fizzled out, Avi comes to her bedroom. Tonight, the door is unlocked. He stumbles a bit and knocks his shin on the bed frame. Shira scoots over to make space.

Their hands hold each other's between their bodies, and they start to laugh, big belly laughs that surely would wake Jackie and Devin up if they weren't so drunk.

Avi's face animated by secret glee. He whispers, "I missed you, Sheer."

"I missed you too. I'm so glad you came back to me."

Shira cannot wait for their next ride. To feel part of it all—the road, the land, the whole world, and to be free all at the same time.

END

Content Warnings by Story

Below is a list of potential triggers and sensitive themes for each story in *Season's Grievings*. While not exhaustive, it's intended to help readers make informed choices.

"Christmas Scarecrow": Transphobia

"All Is Bright": SA off page

"Six More Weeks": Animal death

"Santa Eats Meat": Gore

"Lucy Brings The Light": Fire burns, violence

"The Watcher At Her Back": SA off page

My deepest thanks to Caliope Jade Fuentes for setting up and formatting this book. Her care, talent, and hard work are the reason it looks as wonderful as it does